Clarity

Loretta Lost

ISBN-13: 978-1496021816
ISBN-10: 1496021819

Cover image by Sarah Hansen.

More important than the quest for certainty is the quest for clarity.

- Francois Gautier

Table of Contents

Prologue 1
Chapter 1 10
Chapter 2 24
Chapter 3 41
Chapter 4 54
Chapter 5 64
Chapter 6 76
Chapter 7 81
Chapter 8 96
Chapter 9 113
Chapter 10 122
Chapter 11 127
Chapter 12 139
A Note from the Author 150

Clutching the wall for support, I slide down to collapse gracelessly on the stairs. *What's wrong with me?* I stare forward into the darkness that is my world, gripping the edge of the cold metal step beneath me. I am having trouble breathing. My chest is heaving with short, abrupt gasps; I think I might be crying, but there are no tears staining my cheeks. I have no idea where I am. The dark has never frightened me, but now, staring into the infinite expanse of nothingness... I can't help thinking about death. My mother's death. My own death. Placing a hand on my chest, I try to mentally force my pounding heart to settle down.

Breathe in. Breathe out. Come on, Helen. You're tough.

They all said it would take time. They said that I should give myself time to grieve and get past this. But as usual, I rushed in headfirst, thinking that I was stronger than everyone. I conquer such huge obstacles on a daily basis. What's one more? Of course, I was wrong. I'm always wrong, lately.

"Miss, are you okay?" asks a gentle male voice.

I lift my head at the sound, surprised that I hadn't heard this man approach. He sounds young and innocent—there is genuine concern in his tone. Of course, my tears would choose now to start spilling over. I completely lose all grip on my resolve as my body begins to shake with sobs. I gasp and clutch my knees, trying to fight against my misery.

Just breathe in. Breathe out. You can handle this. You can handle anything.

I feel a large, warm hand resting on my shoulder, and it's instantly comforting. Why is this stranger being so kind to me? It only makes me cry harder. I have been holding on for so long, and keeping this all inside. I just need to be weak for one moment. Just one moment. There is a secret organ gathering pain like a balloon within my chest, and it has been threatening to explode for the longest time. I just need a little cry to let some of the pressure out, to deflate it and keep it from destroying my insides with a near-nuclear detonation.

"What's wrong?" the young man asks. "Can I help you? Anything. Anything at all."

"I'm just..." My voice sounds pitiful and wretched. I take a deep breath and try to speak again. "I don't know where I am."

"You're blind?" he asks me.

I bite my lip and nod. I'm ashamed of the fact, and I generally try to navigate without using the collapsible white cane that rests tucked away within my backpack. It feels like a badge of disgrace, announcing my disability to the world. I don't like being treated differently. I don't like being considered abnormal.

"What's wrong?" he prods. "You look like someone died."

I try to resist, but another sob shakes my body. I am crying again. Just like that; just so easily. I don't have time to mentally insult myself, or try to give myself a pep talk to be strong before I feel the stranger's arms wrap around me.

"Shh," he says, holding me against his chest. "You're okay."

I dissolve against him, completely vulnerable and hopeless. I am not usually this needy, but in this moment, I need to fall apart. I need to accept how brokenhearted I am before I can even try to mend. Just one moment. All I need is this one moment, and I can get back to being me.

That's enough, Helen, says my ever-cautious inner voice. *Get it together. Stop. Stop now. Breathe!*

"Can I help you, honey?" he asks me again. "Anything I can do. Just say the word."

"I don't know where I am," I say again, in a small voice.

"This is the engineering department," he tells

me. "Are you an engineer?"

I release a burst of derisive laughter, and it cuts through my tears. "Do I look like an engineer? Gosh. I'm more lost than I thought."

He chuckles. "Let me help you," he says softly, as he caresses my hand in a soothing manner. He slips my backpack off my shoulders, as if taking the entire weight of the world away from me. "C'mon! I'll guide you wherever you need to go. You need to hold onto my elbow, right? Is that how it works?"

"Yes," I say, inspired by his infectious enthusiasm. "Thanks. My name is Helen, by the way."

"Helen," he repeats, testing it on his tongue. "Helen. What a pretty name. It suits you. You're such a pretty girl."

I smile and wipe my sleeve across my face to remove the moisture. "You're just trying to make me feel better," I accuse as I allow him to help me to my feet.

"Is it working?" he asks.

"Maybe a little," I answer. I'm lying; it's not working. But I do appreciate his efforts. I feel him take my hand and wrap it around his elbow. I am surprised by the size of the bicep that I am grasping. "Do all engineers hit the gym as much as you do?" I ask.

"Only the ones on a football scholarship," he says proudly.

I force another smile. “That’s impressive. I’m a just a psychology major.”

“Psych? Nice. Do you plan on being a doctor or something?” he asks.

“No. I’m going to be a writer,” I tell him. “I just like to understand people. For some reason, I have a class in this building—but I never come here, so I’m not that familiar with the layout.”

“It’s kind of tricky,” he tells me. “Even people with perfect eyesight get lost in this labyrinth. Here, I think I know where the psych class is. Let me take you there.”

“Thanks,” I tell him faintly. I grip the man’s solid upper arm as he guides me off the stairs and through a pair of double doors. He walks at a comfortable pace as he leads me through the halls. Not so brisk that I have to powerwalk to keep up, and not so slow that I feel like a stupid child. I had been a little more than just physically lost, so it is reassuring to feel the strength and warmth radiating through the sleeve of his shirt.

My fingers tighten around his elbow as we make some twists and turns through the building. I am so relieved to be with a competent guide; as prideful as I can be, it does make things easier to be able to rely on someone.

After a few minutes of walking, the boy finally comes to a stop. “Here we are,” he says.

I make a face in puzzlement. “I—I don’t hear anything. It’s so quiet. Are you sure we’re in the right place?"

"Sure. It's just through this door."

Something in his voice gives me chills. My body shudders. I hear the door being unlocked, and there is only a deathly silence on the other side. *Run,* my inner voice tells me. *Run!* But it's too late.

Just as I'm turning away, a hand clamps over my mouth. I lift both of my hands to try to pry it off, but another hand fiercely clinches around my waist. The boy roughly drags me into the room. I try to scream, and violently push away with my legs, but I am held fast.

"Be quiet," he whispers. "No screaming, or I'll rip your tongue out. I'm going to release you, but keep your mouth shut, okay?"

I nod. The silence in the room is deafening. My skin is prickled by rising goose bumps, and my heart furiously pumps hot blood through my body. As soon as his hands release me, I swivel and smash my fist into his face. He roars in pain, and I fling my foot outward, letting my heel connect with his knee. Feeling his leg beginning to buckle and crumple, I quickly duck away from him and lunge for the door. Grasping the handle, I pull the door halfway open before I feel it being slammed shut. The boy grabs a fistful of my hair at the back of my head and uses it to smash my face against the door. I cry out at the sharp pain in my nose, and my lip splits open against my teeth. I taste a bitter, metallic liquid against my tongue. My head spins and I grow dizzy. I feel my body being hauled away from the door and thrown to the ground amid boxes and other debris. I struggle to raise myself onto my elbows to fight against my assailant, but there is suddenly a heavy, crushing weight on top of me.

A large hand clamps around my neck and squeezes. He is suffocating me.

"I can make you feel better, Helen," he says in a tender voice. "Shhh. Just relax. Relax and let me take care of you." I feel his hand reaching down to slip under my skirt. "Relax and spread your legs."

"Are you insane?" I hiss, clawing at the hand he's holding over my throat. He's too strong. Tears flood my eyes once again. "I thought you were nice."

"I guess you missed one too many psychology classes, huh?" he says with a laugh. He leans down and puts his lips very close to my ear. "Just don't worry, sweet thing. You can't see me, so I'm not even really here. Out of sight, out of mind."

"You monster!" I scream hoarsely, struggling against him. "How could you..."

He removes his hand from my neck and hits me across the face. My already bloody lip is swollen and pulsating. I am afraid for my life. Maybe I should stop fighting and let him do whatever he intends to do? My sister and father need me, and I can't die. It would destroy them. They've lost too much already. I can't seem to stop sobbing. I think of my mother. Maybe I should fight with the two-hundred-pound football player, and hope that he kills me so that I can be with her? My mind is a mess. I don't know what to do. I don't know where I am. I don't know if I'm going to survive this.

"Think about calm ocean breezes," the man on top of me says in a soothing voice. "Shhh. My sweet Helen. Think about soft waves of the ocean. Shhh. That's all we are. Soft waves of the ocean."

His sadistic banter chills me to the bone. Why is this happening to me? Why is this happening to me *now?* Why, at my lowest moment, has the universe found a way to drag me down even further—into an even deeper pit of despair? Is this some kind of sick joke? I must be dreaming. This can't really be happening.

But his thumb and forefinger continue to press down painfully on either side of my windpipe. I gasp for breath as he steals the life away from me. This is very real.

"Helen," he coos in a singsong voice as he moves on top of my body. "Helen, Helen, Helen. Such a pretty name, for such a pretty girl. My sweet, sweet Helen. The things I'm going to do to you."

I am not sure what this man looks like, but I

imagine that if I could see him, I would be staring up into the face of pure evil. Perhaps I should be thankful that I will never have to behold something so hideous. *If I survive this*, I inwardly promise myself, *I will have to get stronger, somehow. I can never let something like this happen to me again.*

Chapter One

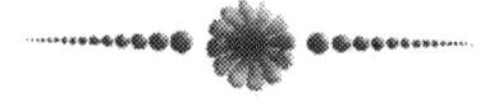

Three years later...

Something does not sound right.

My fingers pause, hovering above the keyboard of my braille typewriter. There is a suspicious vibration in the air this morning, like the incessant whirr of electricity. People always used to be surprised when I asked them to turn off the lights, considering that I am incapable of seeing even the faintest glow—but for me, it was deafening. The city was full of noisy lights that were powerless to brighten my shadow-soaked world, constantly teasing me with their insect-like buzzing. One of the main reasons I moved out here was for the peace and quiet; but at this moment, it is neither peaceful nor quiet. That bugs me.

I hear the sound of footsteps crunching in the

snow, almost a mile away.

Footsteps are not uncommon around here, but they do not usually belong to people. I prefer it that way; I have surrounded myself with acres of harmless, innocent forest, so that my only neighbors are squirrels and birds. They are far more polite than human neighbors, and never dare to bother me—not even to borrow condiments. The trees, of course, have no voices. Unlike in Narnia, they don't whisper my secrets to each other, and mock me when my back is turned. They have been kind, loyal friends—quite dissimilar to most of the people I have known. Anyone who has had the good fortune of spending time with the infinite silence of the trees, will acknowledge their wisdom.

Two distinct voices are approaching my residence.

This is strange and unsettling; there is a flutter of fear in my gut. The only voices that ever come all the way out here belong to the mailman, or occasionally, the repairman from town. I am not expecting any visitors. When I hid myself away in the wilderness all those years ago, I changed my name and did not tell my family or friends my address. I knew they would have come looking for me, not believing that I could manage on my own. They would have continued coddling me, and fussing over me like I was an invalid, and ultimately driven me insane. I have been happy with my solitude. I thought I had escaped the world of prying, controlling, and frustrating people, but these two voices sound self-important and righteous. They sound like the types to callously invade my serenity and toss my life back into chaos.

I am simply not in the mood for this. Pushing my typewriter aside, I rise to my feet and begin pacing in my small cabin. On the carpet, my own light footsteps are soundless and catlike. However, my ears are filled with the cacophony of men's boots smashing the thin layer of ice above the snow, again and again, in an offensive rhythm. I wish they would turn away and go back to their own homes! I wish they would magically turn into tiny chipmunks, scurrying along on their business. I like chipmunks. From what I understand, they are quite adorable. As the male voices approach, I can begin to make out their words—they already sound rude and detestable, and not nearly as charming as chattering chipmunks.

"I swear, Liam. If you made me come all the way out into the godforsaken boonies for nothing, I'm going to be pissed. I could have been relaxing at home with my girl this weekend."

"Come on, Owen! You wanted a special candidate, and she's the one. I'm sure of it."

"But what if she doesn't agree to join the study?" asked the one called Owen.

"Why wouldn't she agree?" countered the

man called Liam. "There are virtually zero health risks! Almost every blind person we've approached has been excited at the idea of being able to see again. There were a few hold-outs... but they were nutcases."

"Yeah, some of these patients with LCA can be real wackos," Owen said. "Being blind messes with their heads. Just don't get your hopes up."

My eyebrows knit together in a deep frown as I eavesdrop on this conversation. Doctors. Why did it have to be doctors? Could it not have been Jehovah's Witnesses or bible salesmen coming to knock on my door instead? Could it not have been girl scouts peddling cookies, or some disaster relief fund requesting donations? Anyone but doctors! Are there any people on the planet as two-faced as doctors? They pretend to care about you, acting sweet and condescending, and as soon as your back is turned, they reveal that they are only self-interested. I haven't had such a scowl on my face in a long time, and my muscles are already beginning to hurt. How did they find me? My name no longer matches the one on my records. LCA, or Leber's congenital amaurosis, is the disease I was born with, and it bothers me that these nosy physicians know about me and my medical history.

A knock finally sounds at the door. "Hello! I'm looking for Helen. Miss Helen Winters?"

I am furious. That is *not* my name anymore. I

consider remaining quiet and pretending that I am not home, but they could come back later. It might be better to send them away with a definitive negative response to whatever offensive query they have for me. They probably just want to poke around inside my eyes and use me as a guinea pig. My father worked for pharmaceutical companies for years, and I know all about the unpleasant nature of such experiments. I knew a few kids with my disease when I was younger. Many of their parents put them through dozens of stressful surgeries and failed research trials, to no avail. I was lucky that my parents saved me from all the heartache of hoping and being disappointed.

"Miss Winters?" asks the man again. "Are you home? Sorry to intrude on you like this, unannounced. My name is Dr. Liam Larson, and this is my partner Dr. Owen Philips. We are currently leading a team conducting some clinical trials with groundbreaking gene therapy…"

"Gene therapy?" I ask in surprise. I had not been planning to speak, but they caught me off-guard. My voice sounds strange and awkward; I have not used it in so long. I am a bit embarrassed that my throat feels like a rusty instrument.

"Yes. We're looking for candidates between the ages of 23-26 to test a modification to an existing drug that has shown great promise. If you agree to join this study, there's a chance that we might be able to give you the ability to see. Would you like to open the door and let us tell you more about our research?"

My mind has begun racing as I stand frozen and rooted to the spot. I place my fingers against my lips to keep from making any strange noises. I don't want to betray how I feel by breathing too erratically, so I try to clear my head and settle my nerves. I have read about recent gene therapy research conducted for my disease, and it was extremely fascinating. Many people were able to regain their sight after the experiments, but there was no confirmation on whether it was permanent, or whether other problems would not arise. Still, I feel an incredible rush of excitement, and my imagination runs away with me. What if I tried? What if it worked, even for a few days? What if I could see all the things I have never seen?

I could see my sister, whom everyone declares to be stunningly beautiful. I could see my father, and finally know what he looks like when he releases that bellow of deep, booming laughter. I remember how prickly his beard used to feel when he would hug me, but my mother always said that she considered his beard handsome. How could something that feels so unpleasant actually be appealing to the eye? What does a beard even look like? Why was my sister always so obsessed with the color of her hair? Why did she struggle to dye it blonde, and then red, and then black? What do those words even mean? What does *blue* look like? I have heard that the sky is blue. I used to dream about supernaturally getting my vision back when I was a child; a fairy would come and grant me a wish, because I had been good, or she had heard me crying and taken pity. The first thing I would always do in these fantasies is run outside and look at the sky, and figure out what the heck *blue* means.

"I don't think she understands what you're saying, Liam," said the man named Owen. He cleared his throat. "Look, lady. We have a great opportunity for you! This gene therapy stuff? It's *astronomically* expensive. So, if you help us now, we'll help you. You can get your eyes fixed for *free*. You could wait a few years for the drug to be approved for general usage—it could be decades—but it will probably cost millions of dollars to get the treatment, and be inaccessible to most people. So, if you let us in, you can ask us questions and sign these papers. We'll be out of your hair in no time. If you're not interested, please tell us so we can leave."

I am not sure why this man seems so rude. Crossing my arms over my chest suspiciously, I am reminded of all the false promises and misleading statements that people have ever said to me. I am reminded of why I left the city in the first place. Dealing with men like this on a daily basis was far more headache than it was worth. Why should I bother? What if I spend months undergoing trials, only to find that it doesn't work for me? What if I never see even the tiniest glimmer of light, even after these doctors have convinced me to be optimistic and to even *believe* that it is highly likely? Why should I overthrow my quiet, tranquil existence for a potentially devastating letdown?

"I don't need your help," I say sharply through the door. I immediately regret the words as soon as they leave my mouth, but my pride is like a snowball being pushed down a hill. "Thanks for offering, but I'm perfectly happy being blind."

"See?" Owen says with annoyance. "I told you this was a waste of time."

The snow begins crunching again as he starts walking away, but I do not hear the second set of footsteps leave. I move closer to the door, and press my ear against the surface. I hear a quiet sigh.

"Please excuse my partner's bad manners," says Dr. Larson. "It's really cold out here and we've been driving for hours. Dr. Philips is just… grumpy."

A warmth and sense of comfort begins to spread through my chest at the sound of his voice. I open my mouth, tempted to apologize. I feel a strong desire to open the door and invite him in for tea. I have not had a conversation with another human being in a long time. I occasionally talk to my publisher over the phone, but it is usually concise and strictly business. Chatting face-to-face could be nice. My imagination starts to run away again, but this time, I keep it in check. The muscles in my forehead have pulled taut in yet another frown. Experience has taught me how this goes; to be fooled by a kind voice and soft words. Buried memories of a haunting deception begin to push into my consciousness. It is always there, chewing at the edge of my mind. Long ago, I promised myself that I would be wary of strangers, and stop trusting my own flawed perceptions.

"How did you get my address?" I ask him angrily. "How did you get my medical records?"

"Your old specialist recommended your name for the trial. Do you remember Dr. Howard? I admit, it was difficult finding you—but I pulled a few strings, and saw that you had some prescriptions sent to this address a few years ago..."

For a moment, it escapes me. Then I remember and swallow in embarrassment. "My anti-depressants," I say, with silent fury. They had been prescribed to me when I suffered a small breakdown after my mother's death. That was absolutely no business of his! Also, unfortunately, the infernal things had not worked.

"Yes. Please, Miss Winters! This treatment could change your life."

I grit my teeth together angrily. "You should not be looking into people without their permission, Dr. Larson. I'm sure you could get in trouble for this."

"Maybe." He sighs again, and I can hear a soft noise, like he is scratching his head. "I only came all this way because Dr. Howard said that you were a really bright girl, and a lovely person. She said that if anyone would benefit from this research, it should be you. She also said you were a writer—she's read some of your books, and was amazed with how much more you've accomplished than most other people with your disease."

My books are my soft spot. I find it very difficult to be upset with people when they compliment my work. I pour so much of myself into those pages, that I cannot help being super sensitive to all acclaim and critique. I press my ear closer against the door as he continues.

"Heck!" exclaims Dr. Larson. "She even gave me one of your books, and it was spellbinding. I'm not a fiction-person usually, but I couldn't stop reading. You've accomplished so much more than most other people, period! People who haven't had to face the obstacles that you've had. You're an incredible girl, and you really deserve this more than anyone. Just have some faith in me, Miss Winters. I promise that I can help you."

I am a little annoyed with him, but my curiosity gets the best of me. "You read one of my books?" I ask him, putting my hand flat against the door. I find myself listening keenly for his answer.

"Yes," he responds. There is a pause. "*Blind Rage*. The revenge thriller. I loved it!"

His words manage to draw a small smile from me. "Thank you, Dr. Larson." My smile spreads through me quickly, and I finally understand what people mean when they describe *fuzzy* feelings in their stomach. It's silly, but the doctor has made my day. Now, if he would only go away before anything more can be said which might ruin my day, that would be ideal.

"You're a smart girl, Miss Winters," he says softly, through the barrier of my front door. "You must know that in 2008, for the first time, there were three research trials done where patients with your disease saw vast recoveries of their vision. My partner, Dr. Philips, is a jerk—but he's right. There's only one gene therapy drug approved for use anywhere in the world, so far. In Europe they recently started making…"

"Glybera," I finish for him. "I know."

"Yes," he responded. "And it's the most expensive drug in the world, costing $1.6 million for treatment. I anticipate that once this drug becomes approved and available, it will be in a similar ballpark."

"That's okay," I tell him, leaning my shoulder against the door. "I'm going to be a rich and famous author someday. I'll be able to afford it, eventually."

"But what about the *time,* Miss Winters?" he asked, his voice pleasing. "You could learn to drive a car! You could get married and have children, and see their faces. See them grow up. That's what everyone with LCA really wants most of all. You could stop hiding away from the world, and get back to society—you could be comfortable around people again. It's easier to communicate and form connections when you can see facial expressions…"

He should have stopped talking when he said he liked my book. This is making me upset. "Dr. Larson, if I wanted to form human connections, I would live in a location that facilitated more interaction. A city or town. Maybe I'd even stay in a nunnery or a brothel. But I am in none of those places. I am in the middle of *a forest*. In *the mountains*."

"That's exactly the problem! This isolation simply isn't healthy for you, Miss Winters. You need to…"

"No!" I shout, pounding my fist against the door for emphasis. "Do *not* tell me what I need. I was perfectly fine before you came, and I will be perfectly fine after you leave. My life is wonderful, and I love my privacy. There are plenty of other deserving people my age, with my disease, who would be overjoyed to be selected. Go find them, and please get off my property, Dr. Larson."

He sighs again. This man sure does sigh a lot. "Okay," he responds, after a moment. "Sorry to bother you, Helen."

"That's not my name anymore," I whisper—so softly I hope he cannot hear me.

This time, I do hear his footsteps departing. They are not as loud as before, and I imagine he must be stepping in the tracks left by his partner in the snow. I wait until I can no longer hear his marching, and finally bow my head in misery at my own self-sabotaging ways. I am acutely aware of the fact that I just lost the opportunity of a lifetime. The opportunity to have my vision returned and be a completely normal person. All because I was too scared to open my door to a strange man.

I had been blissfully lost in my writing only a few minutes earlier, but after this unexpected turn of events, I am in no mood to continue. I consider reading instead. Once a month, I have a few books shipped to my little cabin, and I have accumulated quite the library. However, as I walk over to my bookshelves and caress the braille titles, I feel dissatisfied and disappointed. Reading with my fingers is natural and easy, having done it my whole life, but I have always been curious to see what text looks like. I have always wanted to read a book with my eyes. I have always imagined that the first book I would read, if I ever regained vision, should be one that I had written. But now,

I'll never even see what my own books look like in print. I'll never see the images on the cover, which are "hauntingly beautiful," according to my publisher.

I stumble over to my bed, and curl up under the blankets. I think I will just lie here and call myself *stupid*, over and over again, for several hours before getting back to work.

Chapter Two

I can't seem to focus. My mind is wandering all over the place, and I can't get a handle on my thoughts. I can't sleep. I tried to rest and calm my fretful brain, but after anxiously rolling around in bed for what felt like hours, I can no longer stand the discomfort of this new information. The words are gnawing at my skin like a sudden rash that has covered me from head to toe; neither scratching furiously nor lying completely still does anything to easy my agony. *Gene therapy.* It sounds too good to be true, which means that it probably is. I'm not foolish, and I'm not going to fall for pretty words. Still, the itch has gotten under the protective layer of my skull, and I can't manage to get at it. It's burrowing deeper, and infecting me with promise. *There's a chance that we might be able to give you the ability to see.* Standing up, I begin pacing in my small cabin, moving back and forth across the creaking floorboards.

How dare that arrogant doctor come to my front door and tell me what's wrong with my life? I have carefully designed it this way. I am comfortable in my small, secluded little world. I already tried life in the big city, going to college, and socializing. I tried to be like everyone else, and ignore my disability; but *they* could not ignore it. They were all either too kind and condescending or too sadistic and brutal—there never was anything in between. Why would I want to subject myself to that again?

My cabin begins to feel unusually small. Within a few minutes, I have paced from one end to the other dozens of times. Every lap I complete seems to make the tiny enclosure shrink even further. Now that the doctors have left, it feels achingly desolate here. The once-comfortable silence is now ominous and depressing. I pause in my pacing, as an alarming thought makes my blood run cold.

Am I going to die here? All alone in the middle of nowhere?

Lifting a hand to touch my forehead, I exhale slowly. I'm only twenty-five, but from the way I live, you would think I was an old woman. I bought a hideous, small house in the backwoods of New Hampshire—where no sane person would want to reside. I told myself that this was what I wanted, but if I were to be achingly honest, I would admit that I do miss my family. I miss people. I miss their voices. I miss the simple, comforting sensation of a hug. I haven't had a hug in over three years.

And I just missed out on the opportunity of a lifetime, because I was too scared to open my door.

Suddenly overwhelmed with the realization of what I've lost, I move over to my desk and fall into my chair. My aim is slightly off, and my thigh collides painfully with the arm of the chair before I can find the cushion. I barely notice this injury as my hands begin to scramble over my desk, searching and rummaging for an item that I generally try to avoid using. Then my fingers brush against it; the cool metal surface of my cell phone. I clasp it victoriously in my hand, and rip it out of the wall socket, where it sits perpetually charging in case of an emergency.

Holding the phone close to my lips, my hand shakes slightly. I have been tempted to contact my family in the past, but I have never broken my vow of solitude. However, I don't think I have ever needed human contact as much as I do right now. I need to hear the voice of someone I love. I jab my thumb down on the large, circular button on my phone.

"Dial Carmen," I command. I wait for the cell phone to follow my instructions.

There is a beep of acquiescence. *"Calling*

Carmen! Please stand by."

I take a deep breath. I press the phone against my ear as it begins to ring. I'm terrified that my sister will hate me. I abandoned her without a word. We had been so close, but I had needed to get away with an undeniable urgency. The ringing stops and a rustling noise is heard. I imagine that she might be pulling her phone out of a purse cluttered with random accoutrements. Finally, there is a voice on the other end of the line.

"Carmen Winters speaking! How may I help you?"

For a moment, I am too emotional to respond. A thousand fond memories come rushing back to me, without warning. Her tone is upbeat and perky, with a feminine cadence. There is just a touch of sophistication in her enunciation, so subtle that it might go unnoticed. I've missed her more than I can say.

"Helloooo?" she says again. "Is this some creepy-ass stalker? Because I'm not in the mood..."

"Carm," I say softly. My own voice comes out in a clumsy croak. "It's me."

There's a silence on the other end of the line. I hear her breathing become louder and more erratic. Finally, she releases a sound that is half-sob, half-laugh. "Hel—Helen..." A whimper filters through the line that is somewhere between a gasp and a sniffle. I recognize these sounds. She is trying desperately not to release a torrent of tears.

"Oh, Carm. Please don't cry," I beg her. "Please."

"I knew you'd call me," she says, and her voice breaks. "I knew it! I knew that I'd somehow get in touch with you again, before it was too late."

"Too late?" I ask with worry, my face immediately contorting into a frown. Is something wrong? Is she okay? Dozens of dangerous situations dance across my mind, and I temporarily forget my own issues.

There is another silence on the line.

"Helen... I'm getting married tomorrow."

Now I'm the one making a strange sobbing-laughing sound. "Oh my god! Carmen, really? Tomorrow? To Daniel?"

"No, no. Oh, Helen, you've been gone so long. Daniel and I broke up a few months after you disappeared. I was so depressed, and he just couldn't handle it..."

This news upsets me, and I bite down on my lip. Daniel was a decent guy, and I had liked him. "I'm so sorry, Carm."

"Well, you know. After mom's death—none of us were in good shape." Carmen laughs a little. "What guy wants to date a girl who's crying and moping all the time? And always going on and on about how much she misses her baby sister? But I got past it. Shortly after that, I met Grayson, and he's an absolute angel—not to mention a total hunk. He's really been there for me."

"Are you sure about him, Carm?" I ask her with worry. She used to have a miserable track record with men. I know how she has a tendency to cling to anyone who shows her a bit of kindness. "You're not rushing things?"

"Honey, I'm *29!"* Carmen reminds me, putting emphasis on the number as if it is a critical turning point. "I feel like an old bat. Most of my friends have already gotten married."

"That's not what I asked," I tell her with a frown. "Is Grayson a good guy?"

"Heck, yes!" she says, almost a little too enthusiastically. "He's the one—I'm sure of it. It's going to be an amazing wedding! Daddy is paying for everything."

We haven't even been talking for a full minute, and I am already developing a headache. I am already beginning to remember why I left. I have always felt so inadequate compared to Carmen. She is so dazzling and vibrant, even in her lowest moments. When we were teenagers, and she temporarily experimented with being a blonde, she had decided it simply would not work for her because she appeared "too bubbly." I was confused about how a change of hair color could be so significant, but I never asked for clarification. Most of her fashion-obsessions and idiosyncrasies completely escaped me. Not just because I could not see, but because I could not bring myself to care.

"Helen," she says softly, and her voice is suddenly serious. "Please come to my wedding. Please come home."

I hesitate. There is an odd undertone of fear in her voice, which piques my curiosity and concern. Could something be wrong?

"Please, Hellie," she begs, using the old childhood nickname that had always irked me so much. "It's the most important day of my life, and I need you to be there, standing beside me. I need my baby sister. Will you come?"

I am acutely aware of the fact that she has not asked about me. She has not asked about my whereabouts or my health. Although it's on the tip of my tongue, I find myself unable to spill my own guts to tell her about my infuriating experience with the doctors. I had hoped she would offer a listening ear, but as usual, she is too focused on her own events. Of course, she would be; they are far more momentous and dramatic than anything that could ever happen to me.

"You should be my maid of honor," she tells me. "Please? Helen? I'll get you a bridesmaid dress. There's still time. Have you gained weight?"

I smile. It's the first question she has asked about me, and it is completely ridiculous. "How would I know?" I answer, reaching down to check how much fat I can pinch on the side of my stomach. It's not very much. "I don't own a scale—and even if I did, I couldn't read the numbers."

"Oh, I'm sure you're just as gorgeous as ever, sweetie! Will you come? Please say yes." She pauses, and her voice takes on a somber note. "Please..."

Hearing the wavering sound in her voice, I sense trouble. Scowling, I reach up to scratch my head in disorientation. "I—I don't know, Carm."

"I'll only have one wedding, Helen." Carmen sounds dejected and upset. "It's hard enough knowing that Mom can't be there... but you're still *alive*. Do I have to accept that I've lost my sister, too?"

This guilt trip is working very well. Even though I'm frowning, and trying to be strong and maintain my ground, I feel myself caving. "Fine," I mutter. "I'll try to make it, but..."

"Great! Thanks, Helen! I'll see you soon. Come home as soon as you can, because I'll need plenty of help getting ready."

The phone went dead.

I groan, clenching my fist around the little metal box. "I'm doing fine, by the way. Thanks for asking, Carmen. All that horrible shit that happened to me? Dropping of school? Oh, yeah. I've gotten over it, and I'm living a happy and well-adjusted life. I'm living life to the fullest, really. I have tons of friends. Boys? Sure. There are plenty of men in my life. Most of them are chipmunks, but I wouldn't discriminate." Slamming the phone down on my desk, I roll my eyes and rise to my feet. I march over to my kitchenette and begin ripping cupboard doors open, rummaging around for a bottle that I had tucked away for a special occasion. Or a dismal one. When my fingers collide with the smooth, cool glass surface, I grab the neck of the bottle and yank it from the cupboard. I quickly find my corkscrew, and retire to my small bed to comfort myself with some good wine.

"Oh, you really enjoyed my latest book? Thanks for telling me, Carmen! It's so thoughtful of you to keep reading my work. I haven't been insecure at all. It's not even slightly difficult being a blind writer." I can't be bothered to get a glass, so once I remove the cork, I drink directly from the bottle. The rich, robust flavor of the liquid smothers my tongue, and I lean back against the wooden wall in satisfaction. "By the way, I'm making *tons* of money. That's why I bought a rundown cabin in the wilderness. Because of the hot location—I'm sure my property value is doubling, as we speak. Thanks for asking."

I know that it might not sound this way at the moment, but I love my sister. Everything about her is just so flawless that I can't help but be frustrated; her personality feels radiant—almost luminous. Even her name! *Carmen* makes me think of the legendary heroine in an opera. *Helen* just sounds like a boring scientist. That's why I tried to change my name and leave my old life behind me. But today, the past won't stop hunting me down. I take another swig from my bottle. "Of course I'll come to your wedding! Tomorrow? Sure, that's not inconvenient at all. Let me just get in my fancy car and have my chauffeur bring me over there. It's only two states away—not much of a trip or anything." I take another drink.

I'm in the middle of talking to myself, yammering on like a crazy person, when I hear the crunching of footsteps again. In my surprise, I nearly drop the wine bottle I'm cradling against myself. More visitors? A determined knock echoes against the wooden door of my cabin. I look up sharply, glaring in the direction of the sound. I remain motionless for a moment, staring into the dark expanse of my oblivion. It may be black, but my imagination has never failed to paint fantastic images in every direction I gaze. Even when my eyes are closed, my mind creates whimsical shapes and patterns, dancing and spinning in the empty darkness.

But in this moment, my imagination falters. There is only obscurity.

A stronger knock is heard on my door. "Miss Winters!" says a demanding male voice. "Open this door. We need to talk."

I hug the wine bottle closer against me. I recognize the irritating doctor's voice from earlier.

I am not sure whether I should be relieved or upset that he returned. It is true that I had been clinging to a sliver of hope that I could get a second chance to accept his offer. But now that he is here, I am not sure how to tell him that I might like to try. I have spent so much time running away from people that it is difficult to accept help. Long ago, I promised myself that I would lock myself up and never open the door to anyone. If I were to turn the knob and crack the door open even a few inches, I know that all kinds of danger would pour through that crevice and surely ruin my life.

People can never seem to walk into my world without walking all over me.

They also leave their filthy, muddy footprints all over the floor, which I simply hate cleaning. I realize that most people hate housework, but it's actually very difficult to clean when you're blind. I would like to believe that I have more justification for hating cleaning than the average person.

He knocks again.

"Come on!" he shouts through the door. "I'm a doctor, Helen! You can trust me. I know that you want to be a part of this study. Who wouldn't? Let me in. Let me in so we can discuss this like adults."

Scooting my body into the corner of my bed and the wall, I arrange my pillows around myself so I feel safe and protected. If this is a siege, then I'm willing to wait forever. I am not going to open that door. I take another large drink of my wine.

"What is wrong with you?" yells the doctor. "I won't let you miss out on this opportunity. My colleague gave up on you, but I haven't! Don't you understand how expensive this procedure is, and how valuable it could be? You could have a life, Helen! A real life!"

I frown deeply. *He sure is charming and polite,* I think to myself sarcastically.

"You could see the sunrise," he tells me. "You could see the sunset." He pauses. "Do you remember that scene near the end of *Blind Rage*, where the couple is standing and talking on the balcony in Greece, at sunset? You described such a breathtaking sky, and it just broke my heart to think that your readers were all getting to see the picture in their minds—but you, the writer, could not. Wouldn't you like to know what a sunset looks like? I could show you."

I squint a little, making a face of displeasure. He's using my books as a weapon against me. That is not fair. A sunset is the natural phenomenon that I most desire to see.

"The aurora borealis," he continues. "You've written about that, too. You have no idea what it looks like, Helen. These crazy, mystical lights dancing all over the northern sky. It's mind-blowing. Wouldn't you like to see that?"

I would. I would very much like to see that, and so much more. I clamp my lips together tightly to keep from responding and betraying my eagerness and apprehension. The conflicting emotions are giving me a headache. "Just go away," I whisper. I speak so softly that I am sure he cannot hear me. "Just go away."

"Helen, I can help you. For god's sake, woman! Have a little faith." He hesitates, speaking a little quieter. "I don't know what people have done to you in the past that have made you so guarded, but you need to trust me. I became a doctor so I could take care of people. If you let me, I'll take care of you."

His voice has a strange quality that gives me a tiny shiver. I feel the little hairs on my arms and the back of my neck standing up. It feels like my body is trying to tell me something; is it trying to encourage or warn me? Should I trust this man? I want to. I want to just throw caution to the wind and shout, *Yes! Yes! Fix me! Please make me normal.* However, a nagging negative feeling restrains me. I know that if I accept this offer, something terrible will happen. Something terrible always does.

"Okay, look." The man sighs. "You don't have to agree to participate in our study. But I was really excited to meet you. I came out all this way... and I would hate to leave without something to remember you by." He begins to fiddle with my door. The sound of rusty metal grating against rusty metal is heard.

My entire body tenses up. Is he trying to break into my cabin? I feel my heart rate quicken, and my hands clamp tightly around my wine bottle. The muscles in my thighs become so taut that they hurt. I shrink even further back into my corner, reminding myself to breathe. Finally, a dull thump is heard. The metal noises abruptly stop.

"I just slipped a copy of *Blind Rage* through the mail slot," says the doctor. "Do you think you could autograph the book and pass it back to me? It would mean a lot."

My face contorts in puzzlement. A small laugh escapes my throat. I place my wine bottle down on my nightstand and move over to the door. Stooping down to the ground, I feel around for the paperback novel. My hand connects with the soft, familiar pages. I smile. I can almost feel that it's my book, even before brushing my fingers over the raised lettering.

"Who should I make this out to?" I ask softly.

"To Liam," he responds.

I move over to my desk, and begin pulling out drawers in search of a pen. My hand finally touches a slender cylinder—I do not have much use for pens, so I am surprised that I even have one. I quickly scrawl a few words over the inside cover of the novel. I do not write often, but I have done this many times for book signings. My handwriting is probably not that attractive, but it's the best I can manage. Using my finger to guide my lines, I write a personalized inscription:

To Liam
Please leave me alone.
Winter Rose

With a sly smile, I move back over to the door. I feel around for the mail slot and lift the metal flap, sliding the book through the opening. "Here you go," I tell him. "A special autograph just for you."

"Thank you!" he says with enthusiasm, reaching to take the book from me.

His fingertips brush against mine, and I jerk my hand away hastily. I stumble backward and collide with my desk. Clutching the hand that he had barely grazed, I feel my fingers to see if they have been somehow burned or scalded. I hold my breath, pressing my stinging fingers against my stomach. It feels like they are on fire.

I have not touched another human being in over three years. It's unsettling.

Having read the inscription, Liam laughs lightly. "Wow! Thanks, Winter—uh, I mean Helen! Sorry, I didn't mean to call you by your pseudonym."

"Act—actually," I say haltingly, as I try to ignore the odd sensation in my fingers, "that's my name now. I legally changed it to Winter Rose."

"Well, it is very pretty," he responds, "but I think Helen has a certain charm, too. Why did you change it?"

Pulling my lips into a grim line, I display distaste—even though he cannot see my expression through the door. "I just... I couldn't be Helen anymore. I didn't like her."

There is a silence. I begin to feel a bit stupid for saying something so personal.

Liam moves to sit outside my door, and I hear his back thump gently against the wood. When he speaks again, his words are soft and serious. "It would be a great help if you could assist me in my research study. I really think you're an excellent candidate."

I hesitate before responding. "What if it doesn't work out?"

"It will. I promise that it will be worth the risk," he assures me.

"Can you give me a little more information?" I ask him softly.

"Maybe if you let me in. It's fucking cold out here."

I bite down on my lip as I consider this. Immediately, I feel self-conscious. "Uh, I'm not sure how tidy it is in here. I wasn't expecting visitors, and cleaning can be difficult."

"I don't care," he responds. "Heck, I'll tidy up for you! Just let me in, Winter. I promise you won't regret it."

I take a deep breath. Remembering how lost I felt before, when he walked away and I thought the opportunity was gone forever, I step forward boldly. I reach out and touch my doorknob, tracing the lock with my fingertip. "I'll let you in," I tell him, "but you have to do something for me in return."

"Sure!" he says instantly. "Whatever you need."

I smile deviously. My fingers turn the lock, and for the first time in three years, I open the door to a stranger.

Chapter Three

As the door swings open, I begin to have panicked second thoughts. I try to slam the wooden panel closed, but there is already a person in the way. He walks into my cabin, and I can sense him looking around and assessing everything.

"This is a sweet little setup," he says in surprise. "You're very organized."

I'm a little nervous, so I keep holding the door open, letting the cold air gust into the room. "This wasn't a good idea," I tell the doctor. "I changed my mind. You should go."

"Wow," he says softly. "You're drop-dead gorgeous."

I shift uncomfortably as I imagine his eyes roaming all over my body. I crinkle my nose up in a rebellious attempt to look unattractive. "Well, I wouldn't know. I have never looked into a mirror."

"For that reason alone, you should take my offer," he informs me. "When you gain the ability to see, the first thing I'm going to do after the operation is present you with a mirror. You should know what you're missing. This? What I'm looking at right now? It's on par with your sunsets."

"Ha. You're some kind of smooth talker, aren't you?" I ask with a grumble. Self-consciously, I reach up to touch my hair. The texture is bland and dry; not smooth and silky like my sister's hair. I am sure it looks as lackluster as it feels. I really don't take care of myself and all those superficial details quite as much as I should. "You don't have to butter me up with fake flattery," I assure the doctor. "Just give me the facts."

"Could you at least shut the door and give me a minute to warm up?" he asks me. There is a sound like he is rubbing his hands together and blowing on them. "It's colder than a banshee's nipple ring out there."

"Oh," I muse to myself. "I like that phrase. I'll have to use it in a book, sometime..."

"Helen, please? The door?"

With an exasperated sigh at his childishness, I shut the door with a dramatic flourish. "Is that better, tough guy? Does that make invading my privacy and ruining my workday a little more comfortable for you?"

"I still feel like my hands are going to fall off," he said, blowing on them frantically. "I was trying not to complain, but I think that's the coldest wind I've ever felt in my life."

"Aww," I say, making an exaggerated sound of sympathy. "Would you like a cup of tea to warm up?"

"Sure! That would be great," Liam says with enthusiasm.

I point to the other end of the cabin. "The kitchen's over there. Knock yourself out."

He seems to pause for a moment in surprise, taken aback by my words. "You really are a lovely little lady, aren't you?"

"What gave me away? My hospitality?" I ask sweetly. Gesturing around at the desolate location, my lips curve upward in a little grin of sarcasm. "It's obvious that I'm a huge people-person."

The sound of footsteps echoes in the cabin as he heads toward the small kitchen. "Good God, woman. Do you live on granola bars and protein shakes?"

"Yes," I say slowly, "and vitamins, of course. What more do I need?"

"Where do I begin?" he says, evidently appalled by the sight of my barren kitchen. "How about a good, balanced meal with fresh vegetables and meat? How about some fruit and dairy?"

I lift my shoulders in a shrug, pretending not to care. "It's all too complicated. The things I buy have very distant expiry dates, so they're not likely to go bad. It's tricky enough for me to cook and clean, but leftovers are a pain in the ass. I can never figure out what plastic containers in the fridge contain what, and how long they've been sitting there. It gets annoying when you need to sniff everything and do taste tests... I would rather just be secure in the fact that everything is good to eat. Also, it makes garbage disposal a lot easier."

There is a silence, and I can feel him staring at me again. "No wonder you're so skinny. You don't enjoy food."

"Hey! I love food," I tell him with a frown. "I grew up eating delicious meals—I just can't be bothered to prepare them for myself. It's far too time-consuming and frustrating. I would prefer to spend my time punching away at my keyboard."

"Hmm," says the doctor. "I think that if you could see, your diet would improve vastly. Fruit and vegetables can be colorful and aesthetically appealing; you would *experience* your food a lot more."

"Why are you so judgmental?" I ask sharply. "I have a system. It's a good system. Look around! Everything works. I get my groceries delivered every two weeks, and I consume more than enough nutrients to keep me alive and functioning. Actually, I'm quite comfortable with this state of affairs. I write great stories that lots of people enjoy reading. I am a productive member of society." I put my hands on my hips. "Why are you trying so hard to fix me, when I'm not broken? You act like you're some white knight, coming in here to rescue the damsel in distress from her tower. I don't know if you noticed, but I don't need rescuing. I was just chilling here and enjoying a fine bottle of Cabernet Sauvignon, when you interrupted me!"

"I'm sorry," Liam says quietly.

Truthfully, this is a bit of a sore spot for me. I really do miss having wonderful home-cooked meals. When my mother died, things became difficult for us around the house back at home. Carmen and I were both terrible cooks, and we ended up going out for dinner with our father on most nights. But since I left home, it's been hopeless; I have been living on these bland and tasteless concoctions for the sake of efficiency. My occasional bottle of wine for celebration, or misery, is the most delicious thing I ever consume, these days. I won't allow myself to possess anything else, for it will almost surely go bad without my notice. Most of the time, I don't mind being so unsatisfied; I realize that culinary delights are a luxury, and I didn't move all the way out here for the high life. I just hate being forced to remember what I'm missing.

"You can't really enjoy living like this, Helen?" the doctor asks. "I think I'd go crazy."

"Are you an ophthalmologist or a

psychologist? Stop asking such personal questions," I grumble. "Who cares what I eat?"

"It's important," he tells me. "The whole body is connected. If we manage to give you vision, you'll still need a good diet to maintain your optical health."

I twist my face into a scowl. "So, are you going to give me information on the procedure you want to perform on me? Or are we going to stand around making pointless small talk? Are you going to keep complaining about the weather and my diet until I go crazy and scratch out my eyes so badly that you couldn't possibly fix them?"

He cleared his throat. "I have my documents right here in my bag. Let me read them to you."

I listen to the rustling of papers. "Are you wearing a man-purse?" I ask him curiously.

"What? No!" He seems wounded. "It's... like a briefcase. Why do you ask?"

"No reason. You just seem like the sort of person that would carry a man-purse," I say with a shrug, returning to my wine bottle. I sit on the edge of my bed and take another deep swig. It occurs to me that without the few ounces I had consumed earlier, in frustration at my self-centered sister, I might not have been bold enough to open the door. Dr. Liam Larson does not seem as awful as I first expected, and I am grateful to the liquid for emboldening me. I listen closely to the sound of him shuffling through papers. I am eagerly, yet anxiously awaiting more information on his research study, but I am determined to appear cool and aloof.

"You seemed to know a little about gene therapy when I mentioned it earlier," the doctor says. "How much of this data would you like me to go over? I don't want to bore you."

"Just give me everything," I say hungrily. "I would prefer to hear as much as possible about this treatment before diving in."

"Great," Liam says, clearing his throat. "Well, as I'm sure you know, LCA is caused by a mutation in the RPE65 gene. This causes blindness in patients with your disease, because your eyes can't produce a specific protein which allows you to use retinal, a form of vitamin A, to allow your photoreceptors to convert light into energy."

I nod to indicate that I'm following his lecture.

The doctor continues. "The treatment targets RPE65 by delivering genes directly into the retina. This is meant to sort-of *reprogram* the eye so that it can function," he explains. Liam pauses, shuffling through his papers. "I don't want to mislead you. Unfortunately, this treatment is still in its infancy. We're still in the middle of a trial-and-error process. Many people have experienced improved vision immediately after treatment, but some have experienced a rapid loss of the vision. It only works in the short term for some patients, while others have seen vast improvements for at least three years."

"I understand," I say softly. Being able to see, for even a few years, could be life-altering.

"A few years ago, researchers got really excited and thought this was like a magic cure, but it's not quite so simple. We're trying to improve the gene delivery technique, because it only targets a small portion of the retina at the moment. The old, damaged parts of the eye can poison the treated areas and cause them to revert back to their dysfunctional form." He pauses for a moment, brushing his fingers across the information in his binder. He clears his throat. "The reason I hunted you down is because I looked through some of your tests from when you were younger. There are different types of LCA, but your specific genetic mutation looks like it might respond well to our therapy."

Nodding thoughtfully, I run my finger around the rim of my wine bottle. I know that my disease is rather rare, and there are probably a limited number of potential candidates in my age group. It would make sense that he would choose me based on a recommendation. This allows me to grow a little less upset at his intrusion, and a little less suspicious; only a little.

"Helen, you should accept my offer," he tells me seriously. "I really do believe that these clinical trials are going to yield the best results we've ever seen. We're trying a different, dual approach this time to try to cause more complete healing of the entire eye."

"And what would you need from me?" I ask him.

"Well, we'll need to closely monitor the thickness of the outer nuclear layer of your photoreceptors. This means we'll be using coherence tomography to take serial measurements, quite often. A thinning of this layer indicates degeneration of the rods and cones, which we're trying to prevent." He exhales, and there is a sound like the closing of a binder. "Basically, the main issue we're facing is determining how to create a permanent, safe, and thorough solution. You should do this, Helen. If you agree to participate in these clinical trials... it could be amazing for you."

"Why me?" I asked him. "Why are you bothering to try and convince me? Aren't there others, closer to your hospital?"

"Well, as I told you, I'm friends with Dr. Leslie Howard. You're one of her favorite patients, and she actually gave me your book a while ago. When this study came up, I mentioned it to her, and she became insanely excited and began pushing me to find you and convince you to participate."

"Ah," I murmur. This does make sense. I had always gotten along quite well with Leslie. She was an old family friend, and I had even kept in touch with her sporadically after leaving home. Taking another sip of my wine, I quietly mull over this information.

The doctor clears his throat. "Can I make a confession?" Liam asks nervously.

"Sure," I tell him with a shrug.

"Meeting you... is wild. I feel like I'm in the presence of a celebrity."

Smiling a little, I scoff. "Don't be silly. Because of my books?"

"Yes. You're a little different than I imagined, but I did expect you to love your wine." The doctor laughs lightly. "Why are all writers such heavy drinkers?"

"I don't know. Why are all doctors such nosy pricks?" I retort with a growl.

He chuckles at this, and does not seem to be offended. "Did you know that you're really popular in the blind community? I always tell my patients about you to inspire them. There was a fascinating feature a few months ago..."

"I know, I know. That dumb magazine article on the top ten most successful and influential blind people of 2013. That was just a publicity stunt by my publisher. It's marketing. They're capitalizing on my disability to sell books. Don't believe everything you read."

"You're right," he says. "I shouldn't believe anything without hard evidence. Journalists often get it wrong. And so do photographers; you're much, much prettier than the picture in the back of your book."

I raise my eyebrow. "At this point, I almost want to agree to your study just so you'll stop talking. Calling me pretty isn't going to further your case. Also, I don't really care if I'm pretty; what does that even *mean?* I have no concept of what an attractive person looks like, versus an unattractive one." I growl a little. "Are you taunting me? Trying to flaunt that you can see what I look like while I have no earthly idea? Or are you lying to manipulate me, because I'm actually hideous, and I have no way of knowing that?"

"I was just paying you a compliment," he says defensively. "Obviously, it's a subjective matter, but personally, I find you stunning."

"Yay," I say in a monotonous tone. I take a sip from my bottle again. "Well, I think I have an answer for you. On whether I'll participate in your study..."

"Wait!" he says quickly. "Don't you want to know more so you can make an informed decision?"

"You gave me plenty of information..."

"Just take a moment to really think about it," he tells me. "I don't want you to miss out on this because you're being hasty and prideful. There might not be another study like this in the near future. And it's rare to find one in your age group..." Liam sounds like he's getting flustered.

"I'll do it," I tell him.

The doctor continues to panic. "Think about what this could—wait, what? You'll do it?"

"Yeah. But you'll have to do something for me in return, like you promised earlier." I take another sip slowly. "I need a ride somewhere."

"A ride? Sure, that's easy. Is that all?"

"I need a ride to New York," I inform him. "Tonight"

"New York?" he says in surprise. "Well—we were going to head back there anyway. But Dr. Philips and I have a room booked here for the weekend, and he's meeting family..."

"Tonight," I repeat, unwaveringly. "It's for my sister's wedding. I need to be there as soon as possible. If we could leave now, that would be best."

"But it's at least a six hour trip," he says weakly. "We've already been driving so much today. I'm exhausted..."

"There must be some reason you want me, specifically, for your study," I inform him. I'm bluffing a little, and overestimating my own importance. I'm also gambling on the fact that the doctor seems like a really nice guy. "If you take me to New York, I'll be your guinea pig. You can poke around at my eyes all you want."

He takes a moment to ponder my offer. He

sighs. "Could I have some of that wine?"

"Oh. I've been drinking from the bottle..."

"That's fine," he says, crossing the room toward me and taking the bottle from my hands. He is not standing too close to me, but I can still feel his breath against my face. A subtle whiff of his cologne invades my senses.

I flinch and scoot away on my bed, pressing my back against the wall. My heart rate quickens, and I am suddenly very afraid. He seems nice, but one can never be too sure. My chest feels suddenly very full of a breath that I have been holding. I can hear gulping noises from his throat as he swallows a generous helping of my wine.

"Okay," he says finally, placing the wine bottle down on the desk. "I'll take you to New York. Let me just text Dr. Philips, and we'll get going."

I release my breath in relief. I am glad he did not notice my momentary anxiety attack. "Great," I say in a confident voice. "You're also going to help me pack."

Chapter Four

The doctor grunts as he drags my suitcase out of my cabin. "Do you really need all this stuff? It's like you shoved your entire life in here!"

"I like to be thorough and prepared," I tell him as I step over my threshold. The frosty air rushes at me, slapping me in the face and filling my lungs. The initial shock of the cold fades as I breathe in deeply, and I can't help basking in the refreshing sensation. The air inside my cabin tasted hot and stuffy, although I didn't notice this until I was immersed in an atmosphere of superior quality. The cool breeze swirling around me feels alive—it infects me, causing something to stir inside my bones. All of a sudden, I am feeling somewhat adventurous.

I adjust my backpack over my shoulder, as it contains the most important items: my Braille note taker, wallet, phone, and some other handy electronic devices. I figure that I can get some writing done from the back seat of the car while the doctors drive me to my destination. This doesn't have to be a completely wasted workday. I could still write a few thousand words—or possibly take a nap.

"You packed like you don't intend to return here," Liam observes as I turn the key in the lock to secure my front door. "I don't think you left anything of value behind."

"I like to keep the things I value very close to me," I respond, turning away from my cabin and taking a few steps in the direction of the road. Obviously, I haven't shoveled my driveway, and my winter boots crunch through the top layer of ice and sink deep into the snow. I'm bundled up warmly in a heavy coat and mittens, so the cold does not bother me. I turn to look back over my shoulder toward the cabin where I spent the last three years of my life. Of course, I see nothing. But as I try to envision what it might look like, I begin to feel an odd nostalgia for this contrived image in my mind. "Maybe I won't come back," I say suddenly. "There were many reasons I left home; if those reasons are no longer relevant, maybe I'll stay there with my family."

"What were the reasons?" he asks me.

I shake my head, with a small smile. "No. Nuh-uh. You're not going to extract my deepest, darkest secrets only a few hours after meeting me."

"Don't be so sure," he tells me. "We have a long car ride ahead of us, and I can be very persuasive. I am almost positive I can dig up all your skeletons."

"Pfft." I blow air through my lips in a sound of contempt. "You can dig all you like, but I buried those rotting corpses pretty well."

"Then I'll just have to dig a little deeper," he says gently. "I think I see Owen's car pulling up. Would you like me to help guide you to the street?" He places his elbow against my arm.

Jerking away from him, I frown. My neck flushes with heat, and my stomach churns with nausea. His touch was respectful and kind, meant only to offer me support and direction, but I'm not comfortable with this. I'm not comfortable with accepting help from a stranger unless there's some sort of bargain agreed upon beforehand. Unless I know what I owe him in return. We already have a bargain, and I am determined to never need anything more from him beyond this drive. "I can walk," I assure him. "I'll just follow the sound of your footsteps."

"Why are you so stubborn, Helen?" he asks me. "It won't kill you to accept my arm. I'm a doctor. I'm here to help you, not to hurt you."

"You are helping me," I say with forced cheerfulness. "You're carrying my suitcase and offering me a ride to New York. Isn't that enough for one day, Dr. Larson?"

"I just don't understand you," he says as he begins trudging toward his colleague's vehicle. "All the blind people I have met usually prefer a little more touch in their communication."

"Well, you hadn't met me," I say simply as I stroll behind him. "I don't like being touched. I don't like it when people use my disability as an excuse to fuss over me."

"That's not what I was doing!" he says defensively. He grumbles to himself, but continues moving toward the road. He walks in silence for a few seconds before speaking again. "I think I should warn you: road trips with Dr. Philips can get a little... crazy."

"Crazy?" I say with a mixture of concern and curiosity.

"Dr. Philips is usually very professional, but there's something about long drives that turns him into a teenage boy. I think he used to do road trips with his frat buddies to Daytona Beach for spring break. He's kind of... odd." Liam clears his throat. "Maybe he'll behave himself with you in the car."

"I'm sure it won't be that bad," I say with a smile.

"I hope not. We're a few steps away from the car now," Liam informs me.

There is an unlocking sound as Dr. Philips pops the trunk open, and a little *oompf* as Liam tosses my suitcase into the back of the car.

"Would you like me to help guide you into

the backseat?" he asks.

I am worried that he is going to touch my arm again, and I step back. "No, thank you."

He sighs. "Look, Helen. I work with patients who have limited vision all the time. Almost every day, really. Touch helps them to connect and understand, the way someone might observe facial expressions..."

"Does it seem like I want to connect and understand?" I ask him.

"Not particularly," he responds with disappointment.

"Good." I would reach forward and touch the car, and fumble around for the door handle, but I know from experience that the handles are on different places on every car. It's frustrating, and I am almost guaranteed to look like an idiot while blindly groping the side of the car and getting my hands all dirty. I would rather behave like a bitch than seem like a moron. So, instead, I thrust my chin into the air. "I'm a writer. I like words. If I wanted to connect and understand, I'd listen to the words people say. That's all I really need. Are you going to open the car door for me, or not?"

"I thought you didn't need help," he says with a chuckle.

"I thought you were polite!" I reply curtly, crossing my arms under my breasts. "I don't need you to shove me into the car, but it's customary to open the door."

There is a sound as his hand pulls the latch and swings open the panel of metal and glass. "I really hope we can restore your vision, Helen," says the doctor. "Maybe once you can see how beautiful the world is, you'll be a little less bitter."

"I'm not bitter because I'm blind," I tell him as I take off my backpack and move into the vehicle. I feel around to get a sense of the layout of the car. "I've just encountered one too many assholes, and lost my faith in humanity."

"Then I'll just have to restore it," he tells me with determination, shutting the door and moving to the front seat.

"Hi," says the man in the driver's seat. His voice is not quite as deep as Liam's. "I'm Dr. Owen Philips. I don't have any faith in humanity either. I think I lost it when my buddy Liam convinced me to come out here for the weekend, and then randomly decides we're going back to the city without any warning."

"Sorry, Dr. Philips," I say with regret. "That's my fault."

"No, no. I blame Liam," says the other doctor. "He's got a fanboy crush on you, so he was easily manipulated into doing whatever you wanted."

"It wasn't like that," Liam protests as he settles into his seat and yanks out his seatbelt.

I hear the little *click* as it locks into place, and I am reminded to fasten my own. I can't believe how long it's been since I was in a vehicle. I usually get everything delivered to me, so I can avoid people—I never go anywhere anymore.

"No, it was exactly like that," Owen says. His voice takes on a high-pitched tone of mimicry. "Oh, I can't believe I'm going to *meet* her! She's *such* a great author! I wonder if she'll sign my book?"

"Jesus, Owen. Stop it," Liam says with annoyance.

Owen laughs. "I bet it doesn't help that she's really pretty. Helen—can I call you Helen?" He does not wait for an answer before continuing. "I know you can't see, so I feel obliged to inform you that Dr. Larson is blushing furiously. He is red as a beet."

"I am not," Liam says seriously. "He's lying. If there's any redness in my cheeks, it's from the cold wind outside."

I can't keep a smile away from my face. His voice is so masculine and confident sounding that it is hard to imagine him displaying visual signs of embarrassment. "I'm sure you're not blushing, Dr. Larson."

"Enough with the formalities!" Owen says, as he puts the car into gear and slams his foot down on the gas. The car lurches forward, peeling away from my cabin. "We are going to have fun on this road trip. Helen, just forget that we're your doctors and treat us like your friends. Just feel comfortable to say what's on your mind. This is a safe and judgment-free zone. I'll get started!"

"Oh, no," Liam says with a sigh. "Please don't..."

"Right now, I'm upset," Owen tells us. "I'm upset because I was relaxing in our hotel room, and enjoying this movie I ordered on the TV, when *Liam* texted me that our vacation was over. He said I had to drive over here right away. And I was *really* enjoying the movie, if you know what I mean."

Liam groans loudly. "Dammit, Owen! That hotel room is on *my* credit card."

"It was just one movie, man."

"Yes, but—dammit! You charged porn to my credit card?" Liam asked angrily. "I didn't say you could do that."

"We're friends. I knew you'd help a brother out," Owen says. There is a sound, which I assume is him reaching over to clap Liam on the shoulder. "Besides, I'm sure it shows up as something discreet on the bill."

I lift my eyebrows. I should probably reach into my backpack and pull out my notetaker to begin working, but I am a little too surprised and entertained by the doctors in the front seats.

"Maybe you shouldn't talk about this sort of thing with Helen in the car," Liam says quietly to Owen.

"Why not? She doesn't mind! Do you mind,

Helen?" Again, he doesn't wait for me to answer before continuing. "Since you so rudely interrupted my movie, Liam, and have no appreciation for the art of porn, I'm going to tell you all about it."

"No," Liam says. "Absolutely not. Here, let's just listen to the radio..." He presses a dial on the dashboard and begins sifting through stations.

There is another noise as Owen slams his hand down on the dashboard and turns off the radio. "Actually, this is *my* car, so we play by *my* rules. If you wanted to pick the topic of conversation or radio station, then we should have taken *your* car. But no, your car is new and shiny, and you wanted to keep it all locked up safe in your garage. Let's take Owen's crappy car, because who cares if we put more miles on it!"

Liam sighs again. "Owen, can you please try to act like a grown up..."

"What's more grown up than porn?" Owen asks innocently. He turns back to me, which I can tell from the direction of his voice. "Hey, Helen! Have you ever seen a good porno? Well, silly me—what a stupid question! Since you're blind, let me try to describe what porn looks like."

"Uh," I say awkwardly. "I really have no interest..."

"No, no. This is important. You need to know what you're missing out on! The skin pressed against skin, the bodily fluids slowly dripping down thighs...”

“Oh my god,” I say in discomfort, sinking down into the backseat and clutching my head which is quickly beginning to ache. “I really don’t want to hear this. I was actually hoping to get some writing done while we drive.”

“Sure, sure. But maybe this could inspire you! Just let me tell you about the movie I was watching. I promise; it had a really great storyline.”

Liam grunts with exasperation. “Not this again, Owen. Please, she really doesn’t want to hear about...”

“Nonsense! She’ll love it. So there’s this housewife, and she’s all alone at home. And then she notices the pool boy, who is cleaning their pool without his shirt on. His abs are glistening in the sun...”

I let out a large groan. “Please stop. That doesn’t sound like a great storyline to me.”

“No, no! You only *think* you know what’s going to happen, but there’s a twist! She asks the pool boy if he feels like pizza, and orders delivery. So then the two of them are making out while waiting for the pizza, and when they open the door to see the delivery boy—*he’s* not wearing a shirt! So then the pool boy and the pizza delivery boy...”

“Please kill me now,” I say miserably.

“Only if you kill me first,” Liam responds.

“But if I kill you, then you won’t be able to

kill me!" I say frantically.

"We could try to do it at the same time, but it seems technically challenging," Liam says. "I guess we're just stuck with listening to Owen."

"Will you two stop interrupting me?" asks our driver. "Now where was I? Oh, yeah! The pizza delivery boy pulls out his pepperoni sausage..."

I should have brought earplugs. It's times like these that make me wish I was deaf instead of blind.

This is going to be a very long trip.

Chapter Five

Three hours later...

"...but my favorite was when the schoolgirl didn't complete her homework on time!" Owen was saying enthusiastically. "It was a great piece of filmmaking, because the professor had this dungeon..."

"Hey, buddy," Liam said, leaning forward. "Looks like there's a gas station at that exit up ahead. Didn't you say you were running low? How about we stop and fill up, and maybe grab a bite to eat?"

"But I'm in the middle of my story!" Owen protested. "Don't you want to hear what happens to the schoolgirl? Helen does! Don't you, Helen?"

"Get. Gas. Now." My voice has never been

more deadly serious.

"Sheesh," Owen says sadly, signaling and pulling over to exit. "Fine, Helen; if you insist. I'm disappointed in you. Liam is a spoilsport, but I would have thought that since you're a writer, you would appreciate a good story."

"A good story?" I repeat incredulously. "Owen, nothing you've said in the past three hours has been anywhere *close* to a good story. Listening to you is making my ears hurt. I think they're melting—your words are like acid being poured into my ear canals."

"Hey! That's not nice," Owen says in a grumpy tone. It sounds like he might be pouting. "It's medically impossible to lose your hearing from listening to someone talk about the glorious art of pornography."

I grumble to myself unhappily. "It's possible if I buy a popsicle at the gas station, eat the popsicle, and then use the popsicle stick to gouge my own ears out so that I can tolerate the rest of this trip!" Sighing, I lean to press my head against the glass of the car window. It is cold, and I use it like an ice pack to soothe my aching ear and temple. I really do feel like if I need to listen to one more ridiculous tale of sexual depravity for no particular reason, I'm going to lose my mind. I really wouldn't care if they were *good* stories. "Seriously. I think I'm going deaf. It hurts."

"Well, that's a bad problem to have when

you're in the car with two eye doctors!" Owen says cheerfully.

"Jesus, man," Liam says to his friend in dismay. "It's been hours. You need to stop talking. Just let me put on the radio... please. What's the point of us trying to mend her eyesight if you destroy her hearing by talking about bad porn?"

"Bad porn? Bad porn? Haven't you been listening!" Owen shouts. "I'm discussing the all-time classics of porn! Highly stylized, exotic foreign films! The vintage movies of yore! Indie sensations featuring young, starving artists; endearing and awkward *real* couples who were just trying to pay the rent!"

The vehicle comes to a stop, and I assume that he has pulled up to the gas station pump.

"Honestly," I tell the doctors. "Can someone look at my ears and tell me if they're bleeding?"

"Sorry, honey," Owen says as he unlocks his seatbelt. "We can't help you there. We're only ophthalmologists, and you need an otolaryngologist. We can recommend you to a few good ENT docs."

"Just buy me a popsicle," I command him with a frown.

"Oh!" he exclaims as he exits the car. I feel the vehicle shift with the loss of his weight. "That reminds me of a great porno. I'll tell you about it once I get back!"

"Get me a popsicle, too," Liam says weakly.

Once the door shuts, Liam turns in his seat to glance back at me. "I'm so sorry about this, Helen. I think he's doing it on purpose."

"You should have warned me more," I say with a fake grimace. Although I've been acting horrified, I actually find the whole situation quite hilarious—Dr. Owen Philips is somewhat adorable in a slightly pathetic way. I try very hard to keep myself from smiling at Liam to betray that I am enjoying the eccentric company. "I almost wish I'd spent thousands of dollars on a cab ride," I tell him teasingly. "At least I wouldn't be scarred for life."

"He means well," Liam assures me. "He's a good doctor, and a great friend. He's also really amazing to his girlfriend."

"Wow," I say in surprise. "How does someone like *that* get a girlfriend? Is she human?"

Liam chuckles. "Yes. Oddly enough. He treats her like a princess, but he still makes time to hang out with me."

"I can see that he cares about you," I say gently. "It's been a long time since I had a friend like that..."

"Why?" he asks.

"Can't say. It's one of my dark secrets," I explain cryptically.

"Damn. I wish Owen would stop babbling about porn so that I could actually talk to you for five minutes," Liam muttered. "You're such an interesting person."

"Me?" I ask in confusion. "I'm just your average hermit writer."

"Exactly," he says. I hear a smile in his voice. "I don't know too many of those. You're part of a very rare species."

I look down to hide my embarrassment. I can feel him staring at me; the tension is beginning to grow thick in our small quarters. He is sitting very close to me, even if we are separated by the back of his seat. When Owen was in the car with us, the atmosphere was light and funny. But now, it's dark and intense; it's laced with something I don't understand and don't want to discover. I try to think of something to say to take his focus away from me and my life. "It's just a job," I say dumbly.

He scoffs. "Just a job? Helen, I work with other doctors every day. We heal people, and it should be glamorous; we should feel like heroes. But in truth, it gets... mechanical. At some point, you start to question how important your work really is. I mean, you can heal a person's body... but that doesn't really heal the person. We aren't just bodies, you know? That's where your books come into play." He pauses, and I can feel him giving me an earnest look. "Books are medicine for the soul. They heal the eternal parts of a person."

"Liam," I say in surprise.

"You are a doctor of sorts, too," he tells me,

"except for the fact that your work persists. If a person reads a good book—they become permanently changed. They can't even help it. They can't unlearn what they've learned. It will always be with them. Our bodies all crumble and fade, and we'll all eventually lose our eyesight near the end, along with many other basic bodily functions. But I like to think that even when we're gone, the soul retains some of that wisdom—some of that feeling. What I do is simple science, but what you do is... magic."

"Stop talking," I whisper. "Seriously, stop talking right now."

"Why?" he says, somewhat hurt at the interruption.

"Because I'm pretty sure that if you keep talking like this... I'll have to marry you, or something," I explain nervously. "So just zip it."

"You'll have to..." Liam is repeating what I said in confusion, when his car door opens.

"Okay!" Owen says. "I filled up the tank, and got popsicles. But Liam, you're going to have to take the wheel, so I can play games on my phone. It's very important. And if you don't want to drive, I'm unwrapping your popsicle and tossing it on the ground."

"Fine," Liam says, and there is the sound of crinkling plastic as he grabs the popsicle and gets out of the car.

I am very surprised that this mild level of

blackmail is so effective. Liam really is a softie. I feel the car shift as Owen lunges into the seat in front of me. I flinch when a cold plastic item is pressed against my cheek.

"Your popsicle, as requested, milady!" Owen says happily.

Lifting my hand, I take the popsicle away from Owen. I smile as I begin to unwrap the item, so I can press the sweet concoction against my tongue. Just as I taste the frozen sugar-water, the driver's side door opens and a cold wind blasts into the car. I shiver. "Dammit. I should have thought of something warm, instead. I wish hot chocolate could be converted into a weapon for self-mutilation..."

"I also got us some potato chips," Owen tells us. "That should keep us going for the rest of the trip!"

"Couldn't you have gotten something more substantial?" Liam asks him. "Like maybe some sandwiches?"

"But you love potato chips!" Owen says to his friend in astonishment. "They're your guilty pleasure. You have some tucked away in your office at work, and all over your house... you can never get enough of potato chips. I thought you'd like them."

"I do," Liam says in dismay, "but you could have tried to make me seem a little more mature in front of Helen. You could have avoided sharing *my* dirty secrets with the highly respected author that we *just* met."

"It's okay," I tell him gently. "I like potato chips too. I'm just surprised at how... casual you both seem."

"We work really hard all week," Owen says, with his mouth full of potato chips. "We need to let loose sometime and just be ourselves."

Liam starts up the car and begins to drive away from the gas station. I instantly feel safe. A wave of comfort washes over me. Sliding off my boots, I pull my legs up underneath my body and snuggle deeper into the soft fabric of the backseat. I remember the way it felt to be driven around by my father when I was younger. I remember being cozy and warm as I listened to the sound of my father's laughter, while staring out the glass window and imagining all the things I could not see. I remember my mother describing the landscapes; fields of cows relaxing lazily in the sun, majestic mountains covered in snow at their peaks, and bridges that stretched farther than the horizon out over the ocean. I remember deserts and double rainbows, waterfalls and fire-breathing dragons—well, my mother might have taken some liberties with the landscape. My sister and father would often join in with the fantastic storytelling, but I never minded the fiction too much.

I did become a writer, after all.

Liam's driving is so calm and solid compared

to Owen's. I can't help thinking that I wish I could be driving with him forever. Even if we never get to my sister's wedding, it will have been worth it to me for the trip. I haven't had this much fun in years, and it's so nice to be around other human beings. These two doctors are so silly and nice, and I simply love road trips. Liam's words from earlier come back to me, unbidden, and I try to shut them out. For some reason, the doctor's words really did make me feel special and important. I had not realized that my work had caused such a great impact on anyone. I am suddenly stricken with the realization of what's happening.

Am I really doing this? Am I really in a car with two men I just met, heading back to New York? Am I really going to have a chance at getting my vision back? Could it be possible? Am I really going to see my family? For a few minutes, I get lost in thoughts of my mother and father. I remember how much they loved each other. I remember Carmen's boundless energy and enthusiasm, and how she could never miss an opportunity to insult or tease me. I remember when things were good.

"Tell us a story, Helen." My mother's voice filled my mind. *"You're such a great storyteller. One day, you're going to be an illustrious writer. Blind or not, you're going to take the world by storm. That's why I named you after Helen Keller. She never let anything stop her! Neither will you."*

The memory is almost too bittersweet to bear. I realize that I have forgotten to lick my popsicle for several seconds, and the juice is dripping down onto my hand.

"Oh, that's right!" Owen said suddenly. "I was going to tell you two about the popsicle-porno!"

Liam and I groan.

"No, really, this one's great," Owen says. "You'll never guess where they put the popsicle."

"I really don't want to know," Liam says.

"Helen wants to know!" Owen protested. "You want to know, don't you Helen? Don't you want to hear about how that sweet, sweet popsicle got shoved up someone's..."

"Hey," I said softly, cutting him off before he can assault my eardrums again. "Can you guys both do me a favor?"

"Sure," Owen says, and he seems suddenly attentive. He seems to know that I need him to pause his joking around for a moment.

"Okay," I begin. "First of all, I don't really believe that either of you are capable of considering me a friend."

"Helen!" Liam says in angry surprise.

"Wait, listen," I urge him. "I'm a femalc, and soon I'll be your patient—I also think I'm a few years younger than you guys, although you act like adolescents. I'm also disabled. All of this would allow most people to automatically consider me inferior in several ways; it would be hard for you to consider me an equal. I know how the minds of men work. However, if you are intent on continuing this charade and pretending to be my friend, could you please stop calling me Helen? I changed my name, and I don't like being called that."

The men seem to be sharing an uncomfortable look as they silently disagree with my statement. I can *hear* the way they are looking at each other, and hear them choosing not to argue with me.

"What do you want us to call you?" Owen asks.

"Winter," I tell him. "Please call me Winter."

"Oh! Like the name on your books," Owen muses. "Sure thing."

"I don't know if I can do that," Liam admits. "You feel more like a Helen to me."

"Please," I coax him. "It really bothers me."

"Why?" he asks again.

My lips curve upward into a smile, and I am almost certain he is peeking into the rearview mirror to examine my expression.

"That's another deep, dark secret," I tell him, trying to make light of my own psychosis. I return to gazing out the window, even though the act is futile. I wish Liam and Owen would tell me what's going on outside the car in the world around us. I wish I wasn't too embarrassed to ask. I try to imagine breathtaking landscapes to distract me from Owen's disturbing visuals, and I manage to transport myself away in my mind.

Chapter Six

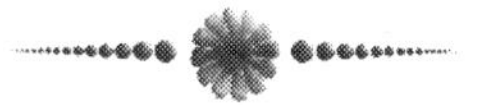

"I'm getting too tired to drive," Liam says gruffly. "My eyes are closing. I'm sorry."

"No worries," I tell him. "I know you weren't planning on doing this tonight. Sorry for roping you into it."

"I decided to give you a ride because I wanted to. You should be at your sister's wedding," Liam says. His voice is laced with sleepiness as he turns to his friend. "Hey, Owen? Can you take over, man? I'm seriously fading fast here. Getting tunnel vision, and everything."

His question is answered by a loud snore.

"Dammit," Liam mutters.

"I wish I could take over," I say in disappointment. "I'm wide awake."

"Do you mind if I stop at a motel, Helen?"

I am a little annoyed that Liam won't even attempt to call me by the name I prefer. "I think I made an error in judgment," I inform him.

"What do you mean?" he asks,

"From the sound of your voices, I would have guessed that you guys were no older than your early thirties..."

"We're actually both in our late twenties," Liam tells me. "I'm 28, and he's 29."

"But you get tired fast," I tease, "like old men."

Liam laughs lightly. "I know we seem childish and carefree," he says, "but we actually do have crazy hours. It's Friday night, so you can bet that we both haven't had a full night's sleep all week." He yawns loudly. "Okay, I can't even make it to a motel. I saw a sign for a rest stop a few miles back, and I'll pull over as soon as I see it. I think Owen has blankets in the trunk."

"A rest stop?" I ask nervously. "Is that safe?"

"It's safer than crashing and dying."

I ponder this for a moment, but as I'm worrying, I feel myself beginning to yawn. I must be getting old, too, for I could also use a nap. When Liam pulls over and parks the car, I am already dozing off. I hear the car door open and close as he moves to the trunk to gather blankets. He opens the door nearest to me and drapes a blanket over my legs.

"Feel free to lie down and get comfortable," he tells me.

"Would it be better for you to come and rest

in the backseat?" I offer quietly.

"I don't want to make you uncomfortable," he says. "I'll be fine in the front." He shuts the door and moves back around the car to the driver's side. Once he gets into the car, he locks the doors and turns the heat up. "Wow, Owen is completely out," he observes as he tugs a blanket over his friend. "He doesn't seem to mind sleeping like this. I think I'm tired enough not to care."

I unbuckle my seatbelt and stretch my legs out on the seat. My feet collide with my backpack, and I reach out to lift it and place it on the ground to give myself more room. I begin to feel slightly guilty that I have so much space while the men are cramped in the front of the car. I assume that they are both far taller than me, and they must be very uncomfortable. I arrange the blanket over my legs, looking awkwardly in the direction of the tired doctors.

"Liam," I whisper, trying not to disturb Owen.

"I wish you could see this," he responds.

I hesitate. "See what?"

"The stars. We're still out in the country, so the light pollution from the cities isn't hiding them from view quite as much as I'm used to. They're just blanketing the entire sky, like snowflakes on asphalt. There's also a little sliver of moon; not big or bright enough to distract from the stars."

"What does it look like?" I ask him softly.

"The moon?" He pauses thoughtfully. "It's like... God's fingernail clipping."

This causes laughter to bubble up in my throat. I touch one of my fingernails to refresh my concept of the shape. I trace the gentle curvature and imagine the moon. "Thanks," I tell him softly, pulling the blanket snug around my neck. "I can see it clearly."

"Good. I'm going to have to turn off the car now," he tells me. "If I leave it running, the battery might die, and then we'd be in a pickle. If you get too cold, let me know."

Nodding, I try to get comfortable. My legs are feeling a little frozen, so I bring them closer to my body. I wrap my arms around my middle, hugging myself. Listening carefully, between the sounds of Owen's snoring, I hear Liam's teeth chattering. I suddenly feel awful for making him do this. I consider inviting him into the back seat again, and maybe moving close to him so that we can both keep warm. The idea makes me a bit nervous, but it's the least I can do since I got us into this mess. As my shoulders begin to tremble violently, I acknowledge that having some body heat near to mine does not sound so terrible at the moment.

"Liam," I whisper again. "Are you sure you don't want to..." Halfway through my sentence, I realize he is asleep. I can hear the change in his breathing. I am saved from needing to ask an embarrassing question, and potentially getting into an even more embarrassing situation. As I drift off to sleep, I imagine countless snowflakes scattered over asphalt. It's an enchanting image, and I might use it in a book someday. I can also picture the glowing fingernail of God, scratching the sky fondly, the way one might caress a sleeping pet.

Chapter Seven

I must have dozed off for a few hours, when a piercing noise startles me awake. For a moment, I'm not sure where I am, or why there's hard plastic digging into my back and making my spine ache. I try to move, and find that my whole body feels frozen. When I hear a man groan, and another curse, I am reminded that I am in a vehicle with two strange young doctors.

The high-pitched noise continues to drone on, and I realize that it is my cell phone. I reach down to my backpack and fumble to unzip it with my stiff fingers. The metal is cold and it makes me wince.

"Answer it already!" Owen says with sleepy annoyance.

"I'm trying," I say as I feel around for my phone. When my hand finally connects with the item, it takes me a few tries to answer. "Hello?" I finally say, bringing it close to my ear. My voice is hoarse and my hands are so cold that they hurt. When I breathe out, I can almost feel the cloud of water vapor hovering around my face. There is nothing on the other end of the line. "Helloooo?" I say again.

The sound of soft crying filters into my ear.

"Carmen?" I say with concern, sitting straight up and at alert. "Is everything okay?"

"No. No. I'm freaking out." She takes several deep breaths, trying to calm herself down. "I'm getting married today. *Today.*"

"Just relax," I command in a stern, take-charge voice. "What's going on?"

"Oh, Helen. I'm just so stressed out. Where are you? I was hoping you'd show up last night. Aren't you coming? I thought you'd be coming."

"Yeah," I tell her, groaning and repositioning my sore body. Liam has turned on the car to begin warming us up, but it hasn't started working yet. "I'm on my way to you. I was living in New Hampshire, so it's a bit of a trip."

"Thank goodness," Carmen says, and her tears abate almost immediately. "I can't wait to see you! How long until you get here?"

"Uh. I don't know. A few hours?"

"Great! Oh, I'm so glad you're coming home, Hellie. I invited a bunch of great guys that I went to school with, so maybe I can introduce them to you, and one of them can be your date!"

"Wait, what?" I say grouchily, blinking and rubbing my eyes. My vision might not work, but my eyes still feel gross after sleeping for a few hours. "A date? Why do I need a date?"

"Because you're my sister! You can't be single at your sister's wedding. Everyone knows that. We need to find a handsome man for you to wear on your arm. There's this guy, Brad—I met him in a philosophy class, but now he's a copyright lawyer. He's very passionate about intellectual property. I figured that you two might have something in common, since he sort of works with books?"

"Carmen, are you insane?" I say angrily, clutching my head. "I don't want to date some douchebag lawyer. I'm coming to your wedding because I care about *you*, not because I want to get set up with random freaks. With your horrible taste in men? Brad is probably a closet serial-killer."

"No way! He's a total sweetheart. You're going to love him. In addition to being Grayson's best man, he's also *so* sexy..."

"No," I say firmly. "Carmen, do you hear me? I swear to God. If you set me up with someone, I'm not coming. I am not in the mood for this garbage."

"But... Helen. You have to come. I told Daddy that you were coming, and he already bought your favorite red velvet cupcakes." Carmen sighs. "I didn't want to tell you this, but Dad hasn't been doing so well lately. He had a minor heart attack..."

"A heart attack?" I repeat dumbly. Remembering my mother's death, my entire body is seized by a panic. "Is he... is he okay?"

"Sure. He's fine, but he'll be better if you get your cute butt down here!"

I shove my forehead into the upholstery of the backseat. "Carm, are you lying to manipulate me?"

"No way, honey. I'm just reminding you of your responsibility to your family," Carmen says innocently. "And part of that responsibility is to date Brad!"

I gnash my teeth together angrily. An idea suddenly strikes me. It's horrible, but it just might work. I glance toward the front seats where the two doctors are sitting, and I bite my lip as a smile begins to transform my features.

"No," Liam whispers. "Whatever you're planning, don't do it!"

I have to ignore him for the sake of self-preservation. "I have to be honest with you, Carmen. The reason I didn't want to date Brad... is because I have a boyfriend. I'm bringing a date to your wedding."

Liam groans and Owen chuckles.

"You have a boyfriend?" Carmen exclaims in shock. "You? No way! Little Hellie has a boyfriend? I don't believe it!"

"Yeah. I didn't want to tell you because... I wanted to surprise you," I lie awkwardly. "He's... uh... he's a doctor."

"Pick me," Owen whispers. "Pick me!"

I am stricken with a mental image of Owen enthusiastically discussing porn with my sister and family. I shudder. There is also the fact that he has a girlfriend, and this makes me uncomfortable—even for a fake date. I don't have many options.

"What's his name?" Carmen asks. "When do I get to meet him?"

I mouth the words *I'm sorry* to Liam before responding. I hope he's not too upset. Shutting my eyes tightly and making a face, I prepare to lie through my teeth. "His name is Dr. Liam Larson. He'll be arriving with me later today."

Owen immediately begins laughing, but he clamps his hands over his mouth to muffle the sound.

"Gosh, Helen! That's so exciting. A doctor! Wow! I'm so happy for you." Carmen lets out a feminine squeal. "So tell me, is he great in bed?"

I start coughing violently. I press a hand over my face to hide my embarrassment. Owen makes a low whistle; he has partly climbed over the seats in order to press his face close to my phone and listen to everything that Carmen is saying.

"Uh, yeah," I say awkwardly into my cell. "He's, uh, really great in bed. Like, the greatest."

"Oh, brother," Liam mutters under his breath.

"How do I get myself into these things?"

"There's a porno that starts *just like this!"* Owen whispers excitedly to his friend.

Carmen sighs happily. "This is such good news, darling!" she says in a wavering voice. "I'm—I'm sorry to have called so late. I know I probably woke you up. I—I just wanted to hear your voice. I'm so glad you're coming. I have been hoping and praying to see you again for the longest time." She begins to cry again softly.

"Carm?" I say in concern. "Are you sure everything's good?"

"Oh, yes. I'm just—just don't mind me. You know weddings make me emotional. I'll see you soon, Hellie? You and your dashing doctor?"

"Yeah. See you soon."

She hangs up the phone, and I do too. I let my head fall into my hands for a moment, as I go over the entire conversation a few times in my mind. I am left with the urge to scream at the top of my lungs, and run out into the forest, never to see these doctors again. "This is so humiliating," I whisper. "I'm sorry. I don't know why I said that. Carmen just gets under my skin."

"Why didn't you pick me?" Owen said in disappointment.

"Liam's more suitable," I explain with a groan. "He's read my books, so he knows a little about me. He can bullshit that we have some previous connection. And also, he's less likely to talk about porn."

"Fair enough," Owen said unhappily, "but I would have liked to be a wedding crasher."

"Is your sister okay?" Liam asks. "Does she usually call you at 5 AM?"

"Whoa," I say in surprise. "Is it 5 AM?" My first thought is that something must be terribly wrong. I consider this for a moment. "It's probably just pre-wedding jitters," I tell the guys, trying to brush it off.

"So you really want me to come with you, as your date?" Liam asks me.

"Yes," I say quietly. "I'm so sorry. What can I do for you in return?"

"Well, since you offered," Liam responds, "I would like some information."

"Information?" I ask with a frown.

"Yes," Liam says. "Remember all those deep, dark secrets I said I'd extract from you? Well, if you share them with us, then I'll be your date for your sister's wedding."

This is probably the worst thing he could have requested. My mouth feels suddenly very dry. "Um. Isn't there anything else you might want? Maybe I could dedicate my next book to you?"

He laughs lightly. "You're going to do that anyway once I get your sight back."

I rack my brain, searching for something I could give him. "I'll have my publisher put out a press release," I offer, "or maybe schedule an event, like a book launch. We can publicly declare that you're the hero who helped the semi-famous blind author Winter Rose to see. Even if it doesn't work, and I can't see, I'll pretend like I can, and you'll probably get tons of research grants and stuff."

"I'm pretty sure that you're going to do that anyway," Liam tells me, "because it's a good story that will sell books."

"Okay," I mumble, getting desperate. "How about I name a character after you?"

"That would be nice," Liam says. "I'll take all of the above, but I'll still need one additional thing to sweeten the pot. Information."

"Why?" I moan in protest.

"Because I'm curious," he answers in a good-natured way. "Come on. It can't be that bad. Tell me your deepest, darkest secrets."

I sigh. "Are you sure?"

"Yes."

"Really? Right here. Right now? In front of Owen?"

"Yeah, why not?" Liam says cheerfully. "He's been telling us way more than we need to know for a while."

"I want to hear, too," Owen chimes in. "Entertain us, storyteller!"

I spend a moment gathering my composure. I smooth my hands over my legs, and look around uneasily. Taking a deep breath, I try to mentally prepare myself for what I'm about to say to two complete strangers.

"Well... three years ago, I was raped."

A hush falls over the car. I can feel the men looking at each other. They obviously don't know how to respond, and the silence is growing tense.

"I guess it's not really a big deal," I say lightly. "I know it happens to a lot of people. I probably shouldn't have let it bother me as much as it did, but it was..." I pause in my narration, searching for the right words. "It was one of the first really awful things that had ever happened to me. I guess you could say I became disillusioned with life. A lot of really bad things happened three years ago." I bite down on my lip nervously. I'm not used to talking about this, and it's difficult to appear calm and emotionless. I just want this moment to be behind me forever. Maybe if I can reflect in an unaffected way, I can finally move forward with my life and be brave again. I look toward the window once more, and lift my hand to touch the cool glass.

We remain sitting in silence for a little while, before someone finally speaks.

"That *sucks*," Owen says unhappily.

"Yeah," I agree with a small nod. "It did suck. I dropped out of school after that, because I couldn't bring myself to go back. I'd had amazing grades, too. I didn't tell my dad or my sister all the details, because they had enough to worry about. I just said I was mugged to explain the bruises and injuries. Actually, the only person I really confided in was Dr. Howard. I knew I could trust her with sensitive information..." I suddenly frown. It occurs to me that Leslie Howard might have sent Liam and Owen to find me out of pity for my situation. While this bothers me, even if it is true, it was still a thoughtful gesture. I try to cast this thought out of my mind. "So, that's my story," I tell the guys, trying to brush it off. "After that happened, I tried to act like things were normal, but I just couldn't be around people anymore. So I moved out of the city and changed my name. And here we are!"

"I'm sorry," Liam says in a low voice. His breathing is ragged, as though his chest might be shaking with bottled rage. "I wish that hadn't happened to you."

I am a little surprised by his tone. He sounds like he cares, and might actually be really upset on my behalf. "Maybe it was for the best," I muse, to myself more than the men. "Maybe it ended up pushing my life in the right direction."

"What do you mean?" Liam asks sharply. "How could *this* be the right direction?"

"Well," I say gently. "I had been working on a manuscript in my free time, but I was so busy with school that I probably would have never finished it. Even if I did, I wouldn't have had the time to look for a publisher. I probably would have kept pursuing my education until I was a doctor like you guys. But after that happened to me..." I laugh lightly at the situation. "There was nothing I could do *except* for writing! I couldn't leave the house due to crippling social anxiety. I couldn't even get out of bed for a while. Writing was the only job where I didn't need enough energy to get dressed and face the world. I only had to face what was inside myself." I hesitate. "This might sound silly, but it's like the universe *wanted* me to write. So it stripped me of my ability to do anything else. I wish it could have been a little less harsh with its methods, but what can you expect? It's the universe."

"That wasn't the universe," Liam says with a growl. "That was some fucking worthless jackass..."

"Shut up," Owen whispers to his friend angrily. "Stop talking about it, or you'll make it worse!"

"How can I make it worse?" Liam asks, also in a whisper. "It's pretty damn bad already."

Owen makes a noise of frustration. "Dude, why'd you have to go and ask her about her secrets? Now you've made things all uncomfortable. We still have a few hours left of driving. Now I'm nervous and I don't know what to say to lighten the mood. Why'd you have to be so inappropriate and personal?"

"Me?" Liam whispers to his friend angrily.

"You're the one who talked about graphic porn for almost four hours. To a girl who's been raped. Did you ever think that maybe the last thing she might want to hear about is kinky sex?"

"You both fail at whispering," I inform them. I hear them hanging their heads like sad puppies. "Guys, it's cool," I tell them, lifting my hands in a gesture meant to tell them to calm down. "I'm over it, really."

"You don't seem to be over it," Liam said skeptically. Something seemed to click in his brain as his voice changed. "Oh. That's why you kept flinching and getting upset when I tried to guide you earlier..."

"Yeah, so I have a few lingering issues," I admit. "It's not a big deal. I've mostly sorted it out."

"Mostly sorted it out?" Liam demands. "Mostly?"

I send him a curt nod. "I'm here, aren't I? I'm taking a chance and going on a road trip with two men I just met."

"But you need counseling," Liam said with concern.

"I gave myself counseling," I explain. "You see, at first, I blamed my disability. I thought it was because I couldn't see, that someone would take advantage of me like that. I thought that it was a weakness; a vulnerability. I thought I wasn't fit enough for society. But I did some reading on the subject, and now I realize that... it happens to lots of people. It was just a random crime. Lots of people commit random crimes, and target people who are weaker than they are. Lots of people like to inflict harm on others, especially if the others seem like easy targets." I give the men a sad little smile. "So, that's why I generally try to avoid people. It's safer."

"That's really sad," Owen says in a depressed tone.

"I don't mind being alone," I tell him. "Writers need their solitude anyway. I think it suits me."

"Helen?" Liam asks softly. "Don't let a few bad apples ruin all of humanity for you. Most of us are good. Most of us genuinely care for others, and don't get pleasure out of hurting those who seem fragile and down on their luck. In fact—some of us thrive on healing others. Some of us will go out of our way to try to help someone we've never met. I hope you'll see that soon. I hope you'll see *everything* soon."

I send a smile in the direction of the doctor in the driver's seat. He says such sweet things, and it's starting to get under my skin more than a little. "Maybe I will," I say in a flirtatious tone, "but for now, let's focus on getting our story straight. I hope you own a tux. How long have we been dating, honey pants?"

"Long enough for you to know that I don't

like being called 'honey pants,'" Liam answers in dismay.

"What do you prefer? Sweet cheeks? Stud muffin? Cuddly bear?" I ask teasingly. "Help me out, Owen. I can't see what he look like."

"Hmm," Owen says thoughtfully. "How about 'handsome tiger'?"

"You think I look like a handsome tiger?" Liam asks his friend, and it's obvious that he's flattered.

I burst out laughing. "I think *you two* have some deep, dark secrets you need to discuss. Now I know what we're going to talk about for the rest of the drive. Owen, do you find Liam attractive?"

"Well, he has these intense hazel eyes," Owen explains, "and when he gets angry, he does sort of resemble a tiger about to pounce."

"Wow! That's really nice of you to say, man," Liam says. He puts the car in gear and begins to drive out of the rest stop. "I'm touched."

"This reminds me," I tell the men, leaning forward, "of a gay erotica story I read once. It started exactly like this, with two close friends and colleagues exchanging a casual compliment that turned into more..."

"I don't want to hear that story," Owen said sharply, cutting me off.

"What?" I say, feigning hurt. "But you shared all your stories! That isn't fair. Don't you want to hear the tale of two athletes, training late one day at the gym? One of them catches sight of his buddy in the showers..."

"Dammit," Liam says. "This is going to be a long trip."

"Maybe I shouldn't have been talking about porn so much," Owen says, wincing.

I smile and proceed to torture them with my words. If my words are the only power I have, I intend to use them well.

Chapter Eight

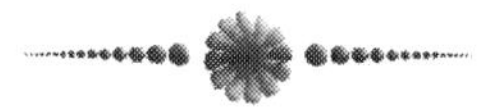

"This can't be right," Liam said in disbelief. "Helen, I think you gave me the wrong address."

"No. This should be the right house," I tell him with embarrassment.

"Jesus. This is where you grew up?"

"Yes," I say shamefully. People often have this sort of reaction upon viewing my childhood home. I hear the men staring at the house in silence. Groaning, I unbuckle my seatbelt and fiddle with the handle of my backpack. I know that I should leave them and go inside, but I'm a bit apprehensive about the reunion with Carmen and my father.

"How many rooms are in that thing?" Owen asked with a gulp.

"I don't know," I say with a shrug. "Fifteen?"

"Fifteen," Liam repeats. *"Fifteen!"*

"Something like that," I mumble.

"Why the hell were you living in a tiny cabin out in the middle of nowhere when you come from money like this?" Owen asks.

"Money isn't everything," I respond glumly.

"She's crazy," Owen tells Liam, "batshit crazy! But it's okay to date a crazy chick if she's rich and pretty."

"It's just a fake date for the wedding, man," Liam said in protest. "Stop taking it so seriously."

"But now you have to make it serious," Owen told his friend earnestly. "You need to seduce her, so you can move into this house and I can come visit you. We could shoot pool. I bet there's a billiards table in there!"

"I'm not going to seduce Helen just so that we can play billiards in her fancy house," Liam tells his friend sternly. Then he hesitates. "But I might do it for the tennis court and indoor swimming pool..."

"Indeed," says Owen. "Think of all the fun we could have! Maybe you could just quit your job and mooch off her."

"There *are* a few television shows I wish I had time to watch," Liam says thoughtfully.

"Guys," I say with mock annoyance. "I'm *right here.*"

"Sorry. Forgot all about you, little lady!" Owen said exuberantly. "I'm too distracted by this big, shiny mansion. Look at those skylights! And the balconies!"

"Even the trees! Even the shrubbery!" Liam declares. "Owen, have you ever seen such perfect, nicely shaped bushes?"

"Yes. Haven't I been talking about porn for hours? I thought I mentioned those!"

I chuckle to myself softly. "Okay, boys. Calm down. It's just a house. You know, those things people live in? It's not really that special."

"Just a house! *Just a house!"* Owen repeats. "Are you blind? Oh—wait. Sorry, it's just a phrase. I meant, like—metaphorically blind."

I make a face at his lackluster attempt at humor. "Thanks." I fiddle with my backpack some more, trying to think of something to say to stall leaving the car. "I just..."

"What's wrong, Helen?" Liam asks.

Blinking, I shake my head. "I have a bad feeling," I murmur, feeling stupid as the words leave my mouth.

"Of course you feel bad," Owen responds. "You feel bad that you're a loaded super-millionaire while your new friends are just poor, struggling doctors who can't even afford a one-bedroom apartment because of their astronomical student loans. You feel bad and want to share the wealth, don't you?"

Liam clears his throat. "Maybe if you had focused a little more in school, you could have gotten some scholar..."

"No!" Owen shouts, plugging his ears. "How

dare you speak that word in my presence?"

"What word?" Liam asks with a chuckle. He raises his voice purposefully. *"Scholarships?"*

Owen lets out a mournful wail. "Nooo! Shut up, Liam. No one wants to hear about you and your stinking scholarships."

Liam turns to me with a chuckle. "I believe someone watched too much porn when he should have been studying."

"If they're playing doctor, it counts as studying," Owen said defensively.

My cheeks are hurting from smiling. These two men have kept me entertained with their outrageous banter almost consistently since we left my cabin. I haven't smiled this much in as long as I can remember. But I know that once I step through the front door of my old house, my smile will disappear. I remember how the atmosphere hung heavy with death and despair, so thick that I could barely breathe. It was my father's grief; he carried it around with him in a dark cloud that poisoned everything. Maybe things will be different now? Maybe now that Carmen is getting married, we can finally be positive and look to the future?

"Are you going to go home, Helen?" Liam asks me. "Didn't your sister need you?"

I fold my hands together in my lap and press them together tightly. "They're going to be angry with me for leaving," I mumble.

"Do you want to drive around for a few more minutes and gather the courage to go inside?"

"No, I should be strong and stop delaying this," I say with resolve. I am tempted by Liam's offer. I would love nothing more than to spend just a little more time relaxing with the guys and making ridiculous jokes. I have only just met them, but they feel like old friends. However, I did manipulate the poor boys into driving me all this way. I can't back out now. "It can't be that bad," I say, trying to reassure myself. "I'm sure things are different than when I left."

"Give me your phone," Liam requests.

I reach beside me to Owen's leather seats, and feel around for a moment before grasping my cell. I extend the small device toward Liam. He takes it from my hand, and immediately begins pressing buttons.

"I'm putting my number in here so you can tell me the details of the wedding," he explains. "You can call or text to let me know when and where I should meet you later today."

"Thank you," I tell him quietly, accepting the return of my phone.

"You can also let him know if your house happens to be infested with giant mutant cockroaches," Owen says with a chuckle, "and he can come to your rescue. Seriously, Helen. From the look on your face, you'd think you were heading into an alien war-zone."

"That's exactly the way I feel," I say with a grimace. I sling my backpack over my shoulder and run my hands over the car door, looking for the handle. "Thanks for driving me, guys. It was really nice of you."

"Well, we made a bargain that helps our careers!" Liam says in a positive tone. "It's a win-win situation."

Finally managing to unlatch the car door, I place one foot outside on the ground. "It was great meeting you, Owen. Thanks for educating me on the wonders of porn."

"Once we get your vision working, I'll have to make popcorn and schedule a movie night," Owen says gravely. "It will blow your mind."

"I can't wait," I say, half-sarcastically and half-enthusiastically. Yes—being able to see anything at all would be a blessing; even porn. The popcorn doesn't sound terrible either, I realize, as my stomach growls eagerly at the idea. My mouth begins to water in yearning for the fluffy, buttery kernels. It is my appetite that finally motivates me to step out of the car; even if there is nothing pleasant or welcoming in that house, at the very least, there will be a delicious meal waiting for me. Not protein shakes, granola bars, popsicles, or potato chips. Real food.

A smile finally comes to my lips. "Well, I guess it's time to go in there and face the music! Will you pop the trunk, Liam?"

"Sure. Let me come out and help you," he says.

"No, no. I'll be fine," I assure him as I walk around to the back of the car. I place my hand on the trunk of the car to lift the lid, but I feel another hand rest lightly on top of mine. I am momentarily startled, but I do not pull away this time. I have grown more comfortable around Liam in the past few hours of chatting.

"Allow me," he says gently, as he removes my hand from the car. "I insist."

A feeling of warmth flushes my neck as I feel his thumb brush against the palm of my hand. His touch is gone as soon as it came, and I hear him lifting the heavy suitcase onto the ground. The sound of the metal sliding against metal is heard as he extends the handle, followed by a loud click.

"I'll walk you to the door," he says.

Reaching out, I firmly take the suitcase from his hands. "You've been a real gentleman, Liam, but I can take it from here. If my sister sees you, she's going to attack you with all sorts of questions. You should probably go home and get some rest."

"Are you sure? I don't mind a few questions..."

"Liam, there's something worse than mutant cockroaches in that house," I warn him ominously. "There's a fearsome creature that no man can ever hope to vanquish: the neurotic Bridezilla."

He laughs lightly. "Do you think you can survive her reign of terror?"

"Sure," I say softly. "It's only one day. I owe her this much, at least—especially after abandoning her for so long..."

"Don't feel guilty for that," he assures me. "It sounds to me like you needed to get away for your sanity and your career. Sometimes, the best thing you can do for another person is to leave. You need to take care of yourself before you can hope to take care of anyone else—you have to shake off all the negativity that's smothering you so that you don't drag others down."

"But I don't know if I'm at that place yet," I confess. "This is so sudden. I was uprooted from my home before I really got a chance to decide that I was ready. I don't know if I can handle this—being in the city again. The air smells different, and it's so loud—even all the way out here in the suburbs."

"Just take it slow," he says. "Take it one day at a time. If you hate it here, you can always go back. I'll drive you myself, if you need a ride."

"Everything's a mess," I mumble. "I don't know where to begin. How do I repair the relationships I ruined?"

"Just try," he tells me. "All you can really do is try."

Although his words are simple, I feel a little bolder. I realize that I am having trouble ripping myself away from him. Kicking the bottom of my suitcase while tugging the handle toward me, I set the heavy luggage at an angle that is easier to roll along the cobblestoned path to my front door. "Thanks," I call over my shoulder, as I begin to walk away. "I'll see you later."

"Good luck!" he shouts after me.

"Liam's really easy when he's drunk!" Owen yells from the car. "Just wear something nice, and make sure he has a few drinks later—you'll definitely get lucky."

I make a face and shake my head as I march along the path to my front door. The wheels of my suitcase rattle and jangle against the cobblestones with a rhythmic drumbeat. It makes the perfect soundtrack for my impending doom. I hear the sound of rushing water to my left, and I am surprised that the fountain in our front yard is running in the winter. It must be because we have family from out of town staying at the house for the wedding. This thought makes me even more anxious. I have never fared well in large crowds.

When I feel the ground become smoother beneath my feet, and my suitcase becomes quieter, I know that I am walking on the concrete closer to the stairs. I slow down my walking a little, and slide my feet along the ground tentatively until my toes collide with the stairs. It occurs to me that I haven't heard Liam and Owen drive away, so I try to be as graceful as possible when I reach down to lift my suitcase, and drag it up the stairs. I count the five steps up to our porch, and place my suitcase down on the flat ground. I suppose the men are waiting to see me enter the house before leaving, and I turn to send a wave in the direction from which I came. If they aren't waiting, or even paying attention, this might look silly—waving at nothing like a fool. However, I would rather risk looking like an idiot than seeming impolite or ungrateful in this moment.

I hear an engine start, and the sound of the car pulling away. I breathe a sigh of relief. It looks like I was waving closely enough in the right direction, and they were actually still waiting for me. It's so hard to follow social protocol when you have no idea what's going on around you. So many assumptions need to be made.

Turning back to the front door, I move forward with a hand outstretched. Beneath my boots, I can feel the fabric of the large welcome mat. When my fingers collide with the stylish beveled glass panel set within in the door, I feel the contours in the design for a moment. Compared to my tiny cabin, this house really was filled with a gorgeous tactile landscape. My mother made a point of making sure that the décor was not only aesthetically pleasing to the eyes of our sighted family members, but also pleasing to my senses. I am surprised when the door shifts under my hand; I am able to push it open without much effort.

Without any warning, a divine scent assails my nostrils. Releasing my suitcase, I walk into the foyer in wonder. I close my eyes and breathe deeply, turning my body around slowly in a 360 degree spin.

Flowers.

I can imagine the softness of the petals and the glorious colors, in tender pastels or vibrant, rich reds. I have no idea what these words mean, but if the flowers look anything close to the way they smell, they must be unbelievably enchanting. I breathe in again, sifting through all the different aromas in the room; I feel like I am pulling apart a piece of fabric and examining each thread. I can just make out the delicate, intoxicating fragrance of jasmine, along with the spicy sweetness of gardenia. Finally, an unmistakable musky aroma; the dizzying and deeply refreshing aroma of roses.

The perfumed air invades my sinuses and lungs, filling me with memories. I recall springtime picnics in the grass, and my mother holding my hand as we walk barefoot through a gurgling brook. I remember my sister laughing and dumping dozens of fresh, velvety blossoms into my arms. I remember pressing my face into the cool softness of the petals, and feeling happy to be alive.

When I was younger, I would rub my fingers over the dresses in my closet, trying to feel the difference in their color. I hoped that there was some kind of special energy in each color that I could grow to sense, if I tried hard enough. But flowers are different—they are alive! They are exuberant to the touch, and they sing loudly to boast of their beauty; you can't *not* see the flowers in your mind when you smell them.

I hungrily inhale the fragrant air, trying to drink in the memories and squeeze every last drop of beauty out of this aroma. It's completely overpowering, and I stand there in the middle of the foyer, looking around in a daze. Have I really stepped into my old house, or did that doorway lead into a different dimension? It has been years since I have encountered a remotely nice smell. I have been content with merely agreeable aromas. But to be immersed in such hypnotic and mesmerizing natural perfumes, all mingling together in the perfect combination for my palate! It's almost unbearable. I almost want to cry at the loveliness of this moment.

I wish I had invited Liam and Owen in to see—but at the same time, I'm glad I did not. The fragrance is so uplifting that it's almost spiritual, and I would not want them to make fun of me; not in this moment. I wouldn't want anything to taint my enjoyment of the lush blossoms. I am almost trembling with gratitude for this moment alone with the posies. I feel like it was designed as a special gift, just for me. I stand in meditative silence for a few seconds, just breathing. I savor every breath.

When I am finally able to form coherent and practical thoughts, I realize that these must be decorations for the wedding. Carmen must have chosen to get married at home! This idea is both comforting and nerve-wracking. I am happy that the big event will take place in an environment that I know like the back of my hand; I won't need to rely on anyone, for I could never forget the precise number of stairs in every staircase, or the angles of every twist and turn of every passageway.

"Meredith?" says a man's voice questioningly.

I was so distracted by the flowers that I had not noticed the quiet footsteps of house slippers on hardwood. I turn toward the source of the sound, and I find myself facing the direction of the library. My father's favorite room. My father's voice. I feel my chest swell with nostalgia and tenderness. I remember the diligent man who was always up at the crack of dawn, working dutifully in that library before any of us had even considered getting out of bed. I remember him reading the best articles in the newspaper to me each morning over breakfast—and sometimes the comics, to cheer me up when I was down. My heart leaps a little, in hope that this could be a normal, happy morning. Like the way things used to be. I have a delayed realization that he has called me by my mother's name. I swallow before speaking, to make sure that the emotion is cleared from my voice.

"No, Dad. It's me."

"Helen?" he says softly. "Heavens, child. I could have sworn you were your mother's ghost. You look just like she did on the day I met her."

I struggle to fight back tears. "Didn't Carmen tell you I was coming?"

"Yes. I haven't been able to sleep since she mentioned it to me," he admits. "But I have also been expecting your mother's ghost to show up for the big day, so I hope you'll forgive me for mixing up our party guests."

Even through my sadness, he is able to coax a smile from me. He seems better than when I left—still wistful and brokenhearted, but in higher spirits. "I missed you, Dad," I whisper, and this time the emotion does cause my voice to break.

"I missed you too, sweetheart." His gentle gait is almost noiseless as he crosses the room toward me. He places two big, warm hands on each of my shoulders. "Let me look at you. My little Helen! You're all grown up."

I nod, lowering my chin to look at the ground. "Dad, I'm sorry that I left..."

"None of that," he tells me kindly. "You were unhappy, and your happiness is the most important thing in the world to me. Now stop moping and let your old man give you a hug."

I don't need to be offered twice. I dive forward, burying my face against his shoulder. His arms encircle me, and for the first time in years, I truly feel like I have a home. I smell his familiar fatherly cologne, mingling with the flowers all around us. I am filled with such a deep joy, that I am almost sure I must be daydreaming.

"Are you going to stay with us, Helen?" he asks me in a quiet voice.

A pang of sorrow strikes my heart, and I remember how miserable and melancholy he was when I left home. I suddenly realize that the man I am hugging does not feel anything like the man my father used to be. His frame is skeletal and gaunt. His arms and shoulders are no longer large and firm with muscle, but wiry with bone. His skin is paper-thin, stretched over his bones like saran wrap.

I am stricken with the knowledge that I could lose him, just like I lost my mother. Carmen mentioned that he had suffered a heart attack. Has she been taking care of him? The big house suddenly feels very lonely. I realize that my father has no one. Even if Carmen hasn't been neglecting him, now that she is getting married, Dad will be even less of a priority to her. He needs me.

"I would like to stay," I tell him softly. "That is—if you're not too upset at me. If you want me to stay."

"Of course, I do!" he says, tightening the

hug. "Who else is going to keep your sister from driving me mad?"

I smile. A pair of timid footsteps distract me, and I pull away from him and look in their direction. "Carmen?" I say with anticipation, but I know that the footsteps sound nothing like my sister's.

"No, no," my father says. "That's our new housekeeper, Natalia. She's here to help out with the wedding."

"Oh," I say in disappointment, realizing that I am actually eager to see my sister. "Hello, Natalia."

"Good morning, Miss," says the housekeeper.

"This is Helen, my youngest daughter," my father says, introducing me with a hand on my back. "She's a writer. She is blind, but don't let that fool you—she's the smartest person in the family, and she will give you much less trouble than Carmen."

I hear the tone of pride in his voice, and I am pleasantly surprised. This homecoming has been a lot less painful than I expected.

"Natalia, will you please take Helen's suitcase up to her room and unpack for her?" my father requests. "I want to have breakfast with my daughter and catch up on the last few years."

"Sure thing, Mr. Winters!" says the housekeeper. "It was nice meeting you, Helen."

I nod, following her footsteps with my eyes. I turn back to my father. "So, where's Carmen?"

My father laughs, a deep-throated rumble. "I don't know what's going on with that girl. She's probably just hung over from drinking too much last night at her bachelorette party. I guess it's just you and me, kiddo."

I frown at this news. When Carmen called at 5 AM, she did not sound drunk or hung over to me. But it would explain her crying and sharp mood swings. I shrug, and decide to question her later about the strange behavior.

"I went to the bakery last night and got some delicious red velvet cupcakes for you," my father says. "Will you join me for a completely unhealthy, sugary breakfast?"

My mouth begins to water, and my legs begin moving toward the kitchen. "Heck, yes!" I am still wearing my winter coat and boots, but I don't even care. I want those cupcakes.

Chapter Nine

I ate five cupcakes. Really. Five cupcakes.

I don't even regret it. They were so scrumptious and delectable that I could have died, right there in the kitchen. Death by cupcake. I could have just keeled over in a seizure of red-velvet-induced bliss. They were, hands down, the best cupcakes in the world. The best substance, period, that I have ever tasted in my life. I didn't even try to be polite. No, I shoved my fingers in there, getting them all sticky and covered with icing. I shed my jacket and kicked off my boots to curl up in one of our upholstered kitchen chairs as I gorged. I stuffed my mouth full to the brim and closed my eyes and chewed very, very slowly. It was heavenly. It was like a celestial encounter with dozens of tiny deities, tap-dancing on my tongue.

My father has been sharing various details of events I've missed over the years, and I'm trying my best to pay attention to him and not to the perfection on my taste buds. It's hard. Most of the conversation does not require my full attention, but I pause and grow worried when he begins discussing our financial situation. For a moment, I am regretfully distracted from my hedonistic joy as I listen to the story of how he lost his job at the pharmaceutical company shortly after my mother's death. Combined with the market crash, our finances were in a sorry state. He had needed to take out a mortgage on the house, which had previously been paid off in full. He complains that he has been incredibly dejected by the looming feeling of moving backward instead of forward. I nod attentively as I chow down ravenously on the cupcakes.

"But things are looking up," he says firmly. "I owe it largely to your sister's fiancé, Grayson. He's a smart boy, with a good head on his shoulders. He's given me some really good investing advice, and it looks like we won't need to sell the house after all."

"So you approve of this guy? He's decent, this Grayson?" I ask, nibbling the icing off the sixth cupcake. The sweetness is finally starting to overwhelm me, and my chewing begins to slow. I inwardly bemoan that I must be approaching my ultimate cupcake-capacity.

"He's wonderful," my father says with a solemn gravity. "I am so thankful, every single day, that he came into Carmen's life. And my life, too. He's been a blessing. He's been a true gentleman to your sister—he's been the son I never had. I am sure that he will also be an excellent brother-in-law to you. I can't wait for you to meet him."

I finish off my cupcake, and sigh in contentment. This news is inspiring. Since I returned home, I have been greeted with breathtaking smells, tastes, and heartwarming news. What more could anyone ask for in life? My thoughts return to Liam. I feel so grateful that he convinced me to participate in his research and helped me get back home in time for the wedding. I can't even remember what I was so terrified about. This is so wonderful. I should have come home ages ago! I can already tell that today is going to be amazing.

And I can't wait to see Liam again.

Something inside my chest flutters a little at the thought, and I feel silly for being so excited. However, it is out of my control now. He said one too many nice things, and I grew just a little too attached to him over the few hours we spent together. While I can strictly enforce my thoughts to be logical and sensible, I cannot keep the girlish giddiness out of my emotions. I blame my childhood home, and the stupid flowers and cupcakes for reverting me to my former optimistic and dreamy state. My mind begins to wander, but I quickly quell the fantasies and remind myself that it's only a fake date. He's going to be my doctor, for god's sake. Nothing can happen there.

But hearing about Carmen's happily ever after is making me crave my own. At the very least, maybe sometime in the non-too-distant future, I could be brave enough to try...

My father chuckles. "If you're finished binge-eating those cupcakes, darling, I'd love to hear about what you've been up to these past few years."

As I gulp down the last bite, it occurs to me that he might be the perfect person to consult about the clinical trial that could return my vision. My father has always known everything about everything. I part my lips, intending to spill my guts and divulge the dilemma that has been bothering me, but then I surprise myself by clamping my mouth shut again. I don't want to hear the downsides. I don't want to be cautioned. I don't want to give anyone a chance to talk me out of this.

I want to hope for the best, even if it's illogical. For the first time in forever, I want to have faith in something. I want to have faith in someone.

Searching my mind for something less sensitive to discuss, I think of my career. "I've written a few more books since I left home," I tell him instead. "Nothing special, just some thrillers.

Conspiracies, spies, revenge, action. That sort of thing."

"That's really wonderful, sweetheart. You'll have to let me read them later."

"I don't think you'd like them, Dad," I say with embarrassment, feeling the heat of a blush in my cheeks. "They're sometimes kind of cheesy, and not that intelligent."

"You're just being modest," he accuses. There is a brief, but heavy pause. "Who have you been staying with all this time? Why couldn't you come to visit? Is there a boy?"

I am a little upset by these questions. I wipe my fingers on a napkin, taking a moment to compose myself before responding. Of course, due to my blindness, he assumes I needed to live with someone so that they could help me on a day-to-day basis. Yes, I am more than a little miffed. "I was living by myself in New Hampshire," I respond quietly. "I bought a small cabin in the mountains, far away from society. I have been living on protein shakes and granola bars, so I haven't really eaten anything tasty in years. That's why I went nuts on the cupcakes."

"Good gracious, child. Why would you do subject yourself to such a life?" he asks in horror.

I shrug awkwardly. "I guess it was what I needed. It was a restorative little reprieve; very nun-like and ascetic. Also, very good for writing."

"You've always been an odd little bird," my

father says fondly.

The old nickname brings a smile to my lips. It erases my previous annoyance. I have always adored my father, even if he often considers me to be mortally weak and incapable of basic tasks. I suppose that parents will always see their children as infants and invalids, regardless of whether they possess any glaring disabilities.

My father's phone receives a text message, and I hear him pull it from his pocket. "This is going to be a very busy day," he tells me as he responds to the text. "The ceremony won't start until 4 PM, but we need to do plenty of preparation beforehand. Guests will be arriving all day. The groom and his family will be arriving around noon. We had the florists come over early this morning, and the caterers are going to start making their deliveries." He laughs to himself. "I should keep you away from Carmen's wedding cake! You might scarf the whole thing down before the guests even get a chance to look at it."

"I think I won't be able to eat a bite of cake," I say, holding my stomach. "I'm all caked-out for at least a decade."

"I have no idea where you put it all," my father says in wonder. He receives another text message, and clears his throat. "You should probably go and wake your sister up," he encourages me. "Please help her out with anything she needs today—she can be quite the fussy bride.

But I'm sure she'll be overjoyed to see you."

"Sure, Dad. I'll try to keep her calm and stop her from stressing out," I say, rising to my feet.

"Wonderful, darling. I have no idea how we got along without you."

When he moves out of the room, I move in the opposite direction, heading for the staircase that leads up to Carmen's room. I do not even bother counting the stairs, or using the banister as a guide. I just let my muscle memory carry me up the stairs, and automatically stop me when I've reached the landing. I am impressed at how flawless my spatial memory is. Even if I'm not conscious of this knowledge, it resides deep in my brain, along with dozens of other secrets that I hope will surface as I need them. It's reassuring to know that my brain is far smarter than I am.

I stroll down the hallway toward Carmen's bedroom. It's adjacent to my old room; while we were growing up, I probably spent more time in her room than my own. I used to idolize my older sister, and try to be like her in every way possible. She was my hero and mentor for the longest while. I'm not sure exactly at what point we discovered that I was actually the more mature one. We were probably teenagers before it happened, but somehow, our dynamic changed. She began to rely on me.

Guilt floods my chest. She relied on me. And I left.

I push these crippling thoughts away as I knock on her bedroom door. “Carm?”

There is no response. I open the door and walk inside, but I do not hear her breathing coming from the bed. I move over to the empty bed and place my hands down on the unkempt sheets. It’s still warm. A muffled sound nearby startles me.

“Carm?” I say again, turning around and listening closely for the direction of the sound. When there is no response yet again, I begin to grow annoyed. “Carmen!” I call out. “We’re too old for hide and seek. Also, you always had an unfair advantage with the seeking part.”

The muffled sound grows louder. It sounds like something between a cough and a cry. I move toward its source, and find myself at the door to Carmen’s bathroom. I knock again, politely.

There is a silence, and some heavy breathing, followed by more strange noises.

“Carmen, what’s going on?” I demand. When I hear the guttural, incoherent vocalizations once more, I begin to feel afraid. I push open the bathroom door. The sound becomes clearer instantly, and I grow aware of the fact that Carmen is on the ground near the toilet, and vomiting into the bowl. I stare in surprise for a moment, before moving forward and placing my hand on her back. “Carm?” I say with concern.

She continues retching for a moment before sighing and resting her face tiredly on the toilet. I know this, because I hear her metal earring clink against the ceramic bowl.

"Hi," Carmen says weakly. "I swear—this isn't what it looks like."

Chapter Ten

"And what does it look like?" I ask her.

"It looks like I'm a psycho with bulimia and I'm trying to ensure that there's nothing in my body so I don't look fat in my wedding dress," Carmen says. "But really, I just drank *wayyyy* too much last night. The girls were just forcing me to take shots, left, right, and center. It was out of control. I'm never going to touch tequila again. Ever."

I lift my eyebrows. "I see that you're still the same old lovable, responsible Carmen."

"Shut up," she grumbles. "It's not fair. If you were around more often, you'd see my better moments. You'd see the highlights. You'd see that I've changed a lot and grown up. But the first time you see me in years, you happen to walk in on me while I'm on my knees and—" She trails off as her body begins to shudder again. She wraps her arms around the toilet bowl and begins to retch violently.

With a frown, I crouch down to sit on the floor beside her. I rub my hand over her back soothingly. I can feel that she is wearing a tiny silk nightgown, and I worry that she must be freezing with her bare skin pressed against the cold bathroom tiles. When she finishes voiding the contents of her stomach, I try to think of something witty to say to distract her.

"Many women spend their whole lives dreaming about their perfect wedding day," I tell her. "Personally, I think yours is off to an excellent start."

"You jerk," Carmen says, hitting me in the arm. "Thanks for being a bucket of sunshine!" She pauses, and her playfulness disappears completely as her voice grows dark and quiet. "Why did I even invite you to come here? It's not like you care. It's not like you want to be here. Why would you? You're so superior to us, and you don't need anyone. I bet you enjoy sitting there and patronizing me."

"Hey," I say softly. "That isn't true. You know I love you. And today's going to be great! Come on, let's get you cleaned up."

"No," she says softly. She clings to the toilet bowl as her shoulders begin to tremble gently with the onset of tears. Her sobs are silent, but filled with misery. "I don't have the energy to move. Go away."

As my hand rests on her shoulder blade, I feel her anguish seep into me from the connection of our skin. Something is really wrong. I remember what Liam said about using touch to understand others. It's too powerful. It's too upsetting and heartbreaking to know that someone I love is so deeply hurt, and that she doesn't even trust me enough to tell me why. I know that it's my fault, and I need to prove that I care about her all over again. I need to be strong for her—today more than any other day.

Sliding closer to my older sister, I encircle her body in a cozy hug. I rest my head on her shoulder. "Fine. Let's just hang out here by the toilet! It's really comfortable here on the cold hard ground. In the years to come, we will often reminisce about this special day, and how you spent the entire morning puking and crying on the toilet."

"I hate you," she mumbles, but when her shoulders shake again, it's with laughter. "You're so stupid, Helen."

I am surprised when she turns toward me and hugs me back fiercely.

"I missed you," she mumbles into my shirt. "You stupid jerk."

For a moment, I just sit with her on the ground and hold her. I run my hand over her hair, and it feels as soft and silky as ever—I wonder what color it is at the moment? Her body begins to relax, and the tension leaves her shoulders. I feel relieved, like a great crisis has been averted. I also feel somewhat... maternal. Tears spring to my eyes as I acknowledge that it's my job to take over Mom's duties in this family. I should have been here to take care of both Carmen and Dad. But instead, I was weak and selfish. I can't be that way anymore.

"You need to get some water and eat something," I tell Carmen, pulling out of the hug and rising to my feet. I reach down to carefully tug on her arms to coax her into standing. "Come on! It's your wedding day. Isn't it going to take several hours to get your hair and makeup done?"

"Only four," she says tiredly as she struggles to stand. She leans on me for support. "Hey, Helen—can you bring me one of those cupcakes Dad got for you? He wouldn't let me touch them yesterday, and I was trying to stay away from anything that might jeopardize me fitting into my dress. But I could really use a pick-me-up right about now."

"Um," I say guiltily, looking down at the ground.

"Helen?" Carmen asks in horror. "Please tell me you didn't..."

"I ate all the cupcakes."

"Fuck you!" she roars, with the bellow of a

great beast about to trample a small city.

I flinch, a little bit worried that she's going to tackle me to begin an all-out brawl. We might be grown women now, and we might try our best to act the way we should, but we had more than a few physical fights when we were younger. They were always great fun. A good rough-and-tumble was always therapeutic in letting off steam. If she needs one now, I am more than happy to oblige—and to take most of the punches so that her face can remain flawless for the wedding photographs.

Carmen growls at me angrily, but she quickly breaks down into laughter. "All of them? Seriously, you ate *all* of them?"

"Sorry," I say sheepishly, and I feel a blush staining my cheeks.

"Psh, whatever," she says in frustration. I can almost hear her rolling her eyes. I know that she isn't really angry, and that she's feeling a bit better.

"You smell disgusting," I tell her, wrinkling my nose, "it's an interesting odor that's somewhere between manure and wet dog. You better take a shower, or your fiancé might change his mind and marry someone who *isn't* covered in vomit."

Carmen giggles and moves away from me to turn on the bath. "Thanks for coming, Hellie," she says softly. "This wedding stuff has been so stressful, and I'm just a pile of nerves. I really needed my sister."

Chapter Eleven

"Are your eyes closed?" I ask her nervously, grasping the hem of my shirt.

"Of course! Just hurry up, we don't have all day," Carmen says with annoyance.

I make a face as I quickly tug off my shirt and slide out of my jeans. I reach for the bridesmaid dress, and grasp it by the shoulder straps before stepping into the garment. I wiggle it up my body, and slip my hands through the armholes before reaching behind me for the zipper. It slides up easily. I move around a little, and the dress feels light and airy, and quite comfortable. "Okay!" I say happily. "You can look now."

"The dress fits," Carmen says with annoyance, "but you lied to me. I thought you said you had a boyfriend."

"What?" I said nervously. "I do."

"Then why aren't your legs shaved? And

why are you wearing *granny* panties?"

"You said your eyes were closed!" I exclaim in horror, covering my body modestly. "And these aren't granny panties—they're comfortable, *normal* underwear!"

"Why did you lie?" Carmen demands. "I'm going to have to set you up with someone..."

"No!" I shout, putting my hands up in a gesture meant to halt her. "Liam's coming a little later, I swear. You'll meet my boyfriend, and you'll see that he really exists! He's just super nice, and he knows that it's difficult for me to shave my legs, being blind and all—so he doesn't mind if I don't shave in the winter. It is winter, you know."

"Do *not* bullshit me, little sister!" Carmen says sharply. I imagine her pointing a finger at me accusingly. "You only ever blame your blindness when you're trying to elicit pity to distract someone from the topic at hand."

Damn. She knows me really well. I had forgotten that. A small smile touches my lips. "Okay, I'll tell you the truth," I say earnestly. "Liam and I—we're doing the long-distance thing. He's a doctor, and he's super busy doing research at the hospital. I need my alone time to work on my books—so it works out really well! We only see each other once every few weeks. It keeps things exciting—builds anticipation."

"Ohhh," she says, accepting this. "That

makes sense. So you *do* shave your legs and wear thongs once in a while?"

"Sure," I say awkwardly. "I mean, my lingerie probably isn't as nice as yours. A little touch of lace here and there." I shrug.

"Good grief. Your poor doctor must be bored out of his mind," Carmen says with pity. She moves over to her dresser and begins pulling out drawers. Finally finding a satisfactory undergarment, she tosses it at me.

"Ow." The tiny thong hits me squarely in the eye. I am not happy about this. There must have been small jewels or metal charms attached to it, for my cheek is actually stinging from the impact. "If I had known that you were going to throw your dominatrix panties at me, I might have reconsidered coming here," I tell her, rubbing my sore face.

"Men are visual creatures," Carmen lectures me. "You need to keep them interested with pleasurable aesthetics. I know that you're obviously *not* a visual person..."

"That doesn't mean you can panty-bomb my eye," I say grouchily. "I might not be able to see, but it still hurts!"

"Just put those on," Carmen commands me. "They'll look better under that dress than the outdated garbage you're wearing."

The novelty underwear is sitting on my bare toes, and I wiggle them apprehensively. "I don't think so. It's not really my style."

"Fine," Carmen says. "Then I'm calling Brad and telling him that you are going to be his date. Since you obviously don't have any real men in your life."

"I do!" I protest. I feel tingles of shame spreading through my chest at how correct she actually is. "I swear, Carmen. Stop embarrassing me. This makes me uncomfortable."

"Then call your boyfriend," she challenges me. She moves over to the bed where my discarded clothes are, and pulls my phone out of the pocket of my jeans. She advances on me and shoves my phone against my stomach. "Call him! Call him so I now so I can see that he exists."

I make a sound of annoyance and exasperation. "Really?"

"Really," she says with severity. "Or else."

Sighing, I resign myself to making the phone call. I feel stupid. This whole situation is very juvenile and high-school, but I need to protect myself from Carmen's whims and fancies. I know that she has always been a magnet for trouble, and has a tendency to drag me down into her mayhem. I do not want to be set up with anyone. I am terrified at the prospect. While Liam is also a stranger, I have somehow grown to trust him a tiny bit—enough to think that he might be mostly a decent human being.

After what I've been through, I have made it

a personal policy to always choose the devil I know.

However, standing there with the phone in my hand makes me a little queasy. I have never spoken to Liam on the phone before, but I will need to be convincing in my lie. I will need to act like we have been dating for a while. I can feel my face growing red at the realization that I have dragged my new *doctor* into this infantile charade. I reassure myself that it won't scare him away or jeopardize my potential treatment—after all, he is friends with Owen. His tolerance for juvenile must be extremely high.

"I knew it," Carmen says triumphantly. "There isn't anyone. You're just standing there with your phone and looking like an idiot. I'm calling Brad."

"No, no," I say firmly. "I was just feeling shy for a moment. I don't really like talking on the phone much, these days." Taking a deep breath, I press the circular button on my phone. "Dial Liam."

"Calling Liam! Please stand by."

I bite my lip as I wait for the phone to begin ringing. It feels like an eternity. And then, once it is ringing, it feels like it's happening far too quickly. The ringing noises come at me like gunshots I can't possibly dodge, and I try my best not to flinch at each one. When a voice finally answers, it's more masculine than I remember and ragged with sleep.

"Hello?" he says with a yawn.

"Hi honey, how are you feeling?" I ask with concern, quickly getting into the character of a loving girlfriend. I press my hand over the phone and whisper to Carmen. "He's been a bit under the weather."

"I'm good," he responds in a husky tone. "Helen? Is that you? Your voice sounds so sweet over the phone. Say something else. I could listen to you for hours."

I feel an odd little ache in the pit of my stomach. I know we're just play-acting, but it feels more real than anything I've had in years. "I'm beginning to regret coming home," I tell him. "My sister is trying to pimp me out to strange men, and I'm getting assaulted with a blitzkrieg of scandalous intimate apparel."

"Let me talk to him!" Carmen says, reaching for the phone.

I step away, keeping it out of her grasp. I am worried she'll ask him something about me that he doesn't know, and figure out that I'm lying.

"Sounds brutal," Liam responds with another yawn. "Do you still want me to come to the wedding? I found an old tux in the back of my closet."

"No, babe!" I say nervously, while dancing away from Carmen's grabby hands. "If you're still feeling tired, you should get some rest. You've been working so hard."

I hear him chuckling on the other end of the line. "I'm guessing your sister is there? It's no trouble, Helen—I don't mind coming to the wedding. I'm actually really excited to see you again! I love spending time with you, and I'd like to do it again as soon as possible."

"I—I miss you, too?" I respond in confusion. For a moment, I am not sure whether he actually meant what he said, or if it's somehow part of our ploy. I forget to move away from my sister's grasp, and she manages to pry the phone from my distracted hands.

"Hello!" she says into the phone. "Is there a real person on the other end of this line?"

I move forward to listen to his responses, but Carmen darts away briskly, and I'm not in an aggressive enough mood to follow her and fight to retrieve my phone.

"Wow!" Carmen says in wonder. "An actual man with an actual penis! You do have a penis, right? And it's healthy? Describe it to me."

"Oh my god," I say in horror, moving to sit on the bed and lifting a pillow to smother my face.

"Lovely. I'm so glad to hear that," Carmen says with approval. "It's great to meet you, Liam. I'm Helen's sister—also known as the bride. Am I going to be seeing you later?" There is a pause as Carmen waits for the answer. "Awesome! The ceremony starts at 4 PM, so just arrive a little before that. Do you know where the house is?" When Carmen pauses again, her voice grows ominous and dark. "Wonderful. Now Liam, I have a few serious questions for you. What are your intentions with my sister?"

I remove the pillow from my face, my eyebrows lifting in puzzlement. Is Carmen being protective of me? I have never seen this side of her, or heard this tone in her voice. It warms my heart to think that my big sister could actually be my big sister for a few minutes.

"I see," Carmen says thoughtfully. "Well, you sound like a tolerable guy. Please be good to Helen. She deserves the best. She's a really sweet, loyal, and intelligent girl. Anyone who can't see that is blind—far blinder than she is."

Warmth spreads through my chest at my sister's kind words. "Carm," I say softly, getting a little choked up. I had forgotten her ability to go from being a shallow, mindless ditz to a sincere and loving human being quite suddenly and without warning.

"Also," Carmen adds, "I apologize for the bleak state of my sister's wardrobe. You'll be happy to know that I'm hooking her up with some irresistible new lingerie that should really spice up your sex life."

"Carmen!" I shriek, launching myself off the ground and tackling her. I wrestle my phone away from her hastily while she laughs, and I growl. Her sentimental mood didn't last for very long. Stepping away, I press the phone against my face, huffing furiously. "I'm sorry about that, Liam." I am relieved to hear that he is laughing.

"Your sister sounds like a female Owen," he says in amusement. "It's too bad neither of them are single—we could hook them up. They would be instant soul mates."

I am surprised at the pleasant thought. "Wow, you're right. They would really hit it off."

"Oh, well," he says in disappointment. "Maybe in another lifetime!"

My face softens. "Maybe," I agree with a small smile. In the brief time that I have known him, Liam has made some rather whimsical and philosophical comments. I imagine him being a lonely person who spent a lot of time with his nose in books as a child. He seems so thoughtful and romantic—especially for someone in the sciences. I wish I had met him under different circumstances. I wish he wasn't my doctor, and I wish this wasn't a fake date.

"So, I made some phone calls. I can get you in for diagnostic tests on Thursday," he tells me. "I want to try to expedite the procedure as much as possible."

"Sure," I tell him, my stomach flip-flopping in excitement. "That sounds good."

"But forgive me—I shouldn't talk about medical stuff today. We should just focus on having fun at your sister's wedding." His voice takes on a roguish and guttural quality. "Are you going to wear something sexy for me under your clothes, *kitten?"*

I press a hand over my lips to try to contain my laughter from bubbling out. "You know it, *tiger."* I hang up quickly so that he doesn't hear me dissolve into giggles at the nicknames.

"Look at you," Carmen says in wonder. "I've never seen a smile like that on your face before. Helen... are you in love with him?"

Her astonishment and questioning quickly returns me to reality. My enjoyment of the ruse is dampened by the guilt from lying to my sister—and the reminder that I am actually just a lonely hermit writer without any friends. "I don't know," I tell her, "but I think I'd like to be."

"I'm glad for you, Helen. I was really... worried. For the longest time." Carmen breathes a sigh of relief. "You have no idea, darling—how I worry about you."

"Really?" I say in surprise.

"Yes." She hesitates. "Hellie? If I ask you something, do you promise not to get mad?"

"Sure," I say in confusion.

Carmen moves over to me, and places a hand on my arm tentatively. "Are you okay? Are you really, truly okay? I just—I always thought... Well, I got the feeling that something terrible happened three years ago. Something more than you were telling us. You really changed, almost overnight."

I turn my head to the left to look in the direction of the wall. I want to conceal my expressions from her as all traces of my smile disappear. "I just took losing Mom really hard," I explain in a distant voice.

She moves forward to hug me. "I know. We all did. Just when you got mugged, and you came home with all those bruises, and locked yourself in your room..."

I clear my throat loudly, pulling out of her hug and standing up. "Hey, isn't it time for your hair and makeup? Won't your photographer be here soon? I should probably go and shave my legs."

"Yes!" she shouts. "Get rid of that forest, fast. If you need help, give me a shout."

"Pfft," I say in contempt. "I can shave by touch quite easily. I just like to complain because I'm lazy. You know that."

She laughs lightly. "I've missed you, little sister. I can't wait to meet your doctor—and I can't wait for you to meet my fiancé! I'm not usually separated from him for this long, but we're doing that whole traditional thing where the bride and groom don't see each other for a little while before the wedding. It's supposed to make it more magical and emotional when we see each other again later today."

"Sounds romantic," I say with a yawn.

"Don't make fun of me," she says, shoving me a little. "You'll understand someday. Now go and get ready." She stoops to pick something up, and hooks it over my arm. "And for heaven's sake, *wear the thong.*"

Chapter Twelve

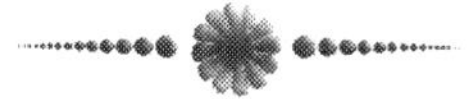

"I thought that *I* was going to be your maid of honor," says Carmen's friend jealously. Her voice is small and whiny, and it's unpleasant being in the same room with her.

"Yes, but that's before I knew Helen would be coming home," Carmen explains. "I'm sorry, Sabrina. She's my sister."

I feel a little embarrassed for stealing the poor girl's joyful moment. She must not have too many. Shifting in my chair, with my ultra-soft, newly shaved legs rubbing against each other, I allow the makeup artist to apply foundation to my face. I feel the fabric of Carmen's thong nestling into my bottom, and it does somehow give me an odd burst of confidence. "I haven't been around for a while, and I don't want to step on anyone's toes," I say as the makeup artist dusts blush across my cheekbones. "Sabrina can be the maid of honor if she wants."

"But I'm the bride, and I want you, Helen," Carmen insists. I hear the click of a curling iron releasing a section of her hair. She makes a noise of frustration. "Where's Emma? She should be here by now."

"Oh, didn't you hear?" Sabrina asks in the gossipy tone of a schoolgirl. "Emma's having some issues."

"Issues?" Carmen repeats with concern. "She didn't tell me anything. Is she going to miss my wedding?"

"I don't think so, but she might be late." Sabrina sighs. "Haven't you heard? She caught Jacob cheating on her a few days ago. They've been fighting since then, but she finally decided to move out this morning. They're getting a divorce."

"No way," Carmen whispers. "Jacob and Emma split up? But they've been together since high school. They're the best couple I know."

"I guess none of us are safe," Sabrina laments. "Frankly, I don't know why you're getting married at all. Shit's just going to go horribly wrong. It always does."

I simply cannot believe how dumb and insensitive Sabrina is being. As the makeup artist deftly applies my eye shadow, I try very hard to keep from interjecting and yelling at the annoying woman. It's clear to see that Carmen is under enough pressure, without stressing her out more about her impending wedding. I can hear the catch in my sister's breathing, indicating that she is about to begin hyperventilating.

"I can't... I can't..." Carmen pulls her hair out of her curling iron and the barrel clicks shut. She tosses it onto her dresser, and it clatters to a halt. Standing up, she begins to pace and tries to calm her breathing. "I can't believe he'd do that to her. Why? Jacob has always been the sweetest guy."

"Who knows why men do half the things they do?" Sabrina mutters callously. "They all end up revealing their true colors eventually."

"Oh god," Carmen moans. "Oh god, what am I doing? I'm not ready. This is crazy. I'm going to ruin my whole life..."

"Hey, hey," I tell her softly, holding my hand up to instruct the makeup artist to pause. I am sorely vexed with Sabrina for aggravating my sister. "It's going to be fine, Carm. I don't know your fiancé, but from what you've told me, he sounds like the type of guy who would never hurt you like that."

"I don't know," Sabrina says skeptically. "Jacob and Emma were together for twelve years, and we all thought they were solid. If they can fall apart so easily, then nothing's safe."

Carmen takes several quick, shallow breaths. "Get Grayson. Please. I'm freaking out."

"What?" Sabrina says with a frown. "But you haven't finished your hair and makeup yet, or even put on your dress. It will ruin your first look."

"Fuck the first look!" Carmen shouts. "I need to see Grayson. Now. Please, Sabby. He should be here by now. Will you go get him? I need to see my man. I need to remember why I'm doing this."

Sabrina makes a sound of displeasure. "At least get your dress on first. This destroys a perfectly good tradition."

"I really don't care about tradition right now," Carmen says, as she struggles to breathe.

Pushing my makeup artist aside slightly, I move over to my sister and touch her arm. "Hey," I tell her softly. "It's going to be fine, Carm. You're going to be happy."

"What if—what if something goes wrong?" Carmen demands. "Almost half of all marriages end up in divorce. What if I end up being another statistic?"

"You won't," I tell her firmly. "You're too smart. You're too funny, beautiful, and amazing. Any guy would be an idiot to let you get away. Come on, Carm. Pull it together." I grasp her wrists gently and squeeze them in a reassuring way.

"I'm going to cry," she says with a small, derisive laugh at herself. "I can't do this, Helen. I want it so badly, but I'm just not ready."

"Forget Grayson," Sabrina says solemnly. "What you need is a drink! Shall I get us a bottle of champagne to sip on while we get ready?"

"No," Carmen says. "I need *him*. I need my

fiancé. If you don't bring him for me, I'll go to him myself."

"No, no," Sabrina says in disappointment. "I'll go find Grayson. Just put on your dress!"

When Sabrina leaves the room, I breathe a sigh of relief. "God, Carm! Didn't you have any better choices for women to have as bridesmaids?" I ask her.

"You might find this hard to believe," she tells me, "but I actually don't have too many female friends. I can't deal with how catty and superficial they are. They're also always jealous, for one reason or another. Sabrina and Emma were just going to be there to make it look like I'm not a total loser."

I smile at this. I do know that while other women tend to be attracted to Carmen, and while she is polite and friendly to most of them, she keeps them at an arm's length. "Let's get you into that dress," I tell her.

"Okay," she says anxiously, moving across the room to retrieve it from its plastic packaging. She heads toward the bathroom to change so that the makeup artists and hair stylist won't see her nude. "I guess this is really happening," she murmurs.

"What kind of dress is it?" I ask as I follow her across the room.

"It's a strapless mermaid-style gown," she tells me, closing the bathroom door behind us. I can hear her running her hand over the embroidery. "I wish you could see it. It's covered in pearls and Swarovski crystals. It's really something."

"I bet you'll be unforgettable," I tell her with confidence. "Now put it on!"

A rustling is heard as she fumbles with the material. She thrusts the dress into my hands.

"Hold this for a moment," she tells me as she unties her robe and steps barefoot onto the ground.

I feel Carmen unzip the dress in my hands and step into it, and I help to lift the heavy garment around her body.

"Oh, I'm feeling better already," she says with a sigh of contentment. "Will you zip me up?"

When she turns around, I brush my hands over the gown, searching for the zipper. When I finally locate it, I begin tugging it up. I am surprised when it gets stuck near her lower back. Biting down on my lip, I try again. The zipper won't go up. I grasp the sides of the fabric and pull them closer together, before trying to zip once more. A frown settles on my face.

"It doesn't fit?" Carmen asks me in alarm. "God. Did I get too fat?"

"Put your arms straight up and stretch your body out," I instruct her. She follows my directions, and with some gentle pulling and tugging, coaxing the zipper up and down, it finally travels up the length of her back.

"Oh my god," she breathes. "I was seconds away from having a full-blown panic attack."

"Pfft," I say in dismissal. "You're fine. It's a good thing you didn't have any cupcakes, though."

"Helen..." she begins saying softly. Her voice is breaking like she might cry.

A knock sounds on the bathroom door. "Miss Winters, we really need to get back to doing your hair and makeup," says the makeup artist. "We're running out of time before the wedding photographs."

"Okay! Be right out!" Carmen shouts, before turning back to me. She sniffles, as though trying very hard to fight back her tears. "Helen, I just—"

"What is it?" I ask her.

"I—I need a Tylenol," Carmen grumbles, moving over to the medicine cabinet. She is struggling to open the cap on the bottle when a male voice is heard coming from her bedroom, she abruptly drops the container of pills into the sink.

"Carmen?" says the man's soft and tender voice.

My blood runs cold.

"Are you here, honey?" he asks gently. "I couldn't wait to see you either."

I stumble back against the bathroom wall, my face frozen.

"Oh, thank god!" Carmen says. "He's here. Helen, you have to meet my fiancé!"

My heart is pounding like a stampede within

my chest. There are a thousand beasts racing across the savannah of my insides, spurred on by crushing fear. My mind has trouble forming logical thoughts, as my body reacts in sheer terror. No. This isn't possible. Prickles of hot panic spread through my neck and spine. A thin film of cool sweat has instantly covered my freshly showered skin from head to toe.

"Gray!" Carmen whispers as she runs out of the bathroom in her wedding dress, and throws herself into her fiancé's arms. I hear her dissolving into tears. "I've missed you," she sobs. "I missed you so much."

I hear him catch her and plant a kiss on her lips. "I've missed you more, darling. Let's make sure that's the last night we ever spend apart."

I feel like I'm going to throw up. This can't be right. I have heard that people have doppelgangers who look almost identical to them—perhaps Grayson's voice just happens to be very similar to the voice that haunts my nightmares. It's highly unlikely that he is who I believe he is...

The sound of Carmen's crying filters into the bathroom.

"Shhhhh," says Grayson in a soothing voice. "Just relax, honey. I'm here."

"It's been so hard—I'm freaking out about everything," Carmen says through her tears.

For a moment, I almost can convince myself

that this isn't really happening. If my sister loves this man, he must be a good person. There is no possible way that he is the monster who...

"Think about calm ocean breezes," Grayson tells her in a soft and melodic whisper. "Shhh, Carmen. My beloved Carmen." He runs his hand over her back and presses a kiss against her forehead. "Think about soft waves of the ocean. Shhh. That's all we are. Soft waves of the ocean."

Something explodes inside me. I see red.

Although I can see nothing, I see everything. Everything is red.

I lunge forward and slam the bathroom door shut before the man can see me. I lock the door. Staggering back into the bathroom, I reach out and grasp for something, anything to give me support. Everything is spinning, and I cannot stand.

I grasp the shower curtain and tear it off the hooks as I fall to my knees. I hit my head on the ceramic edge of the tub, but I barely notice this due to the pain, dizziness, and nausea that has already seized my body. I press my face into the folds of the shower curtain, and scream. I scream at the top of my lungs. I scream bloody murder. I scream with years of pent up fury.

But no sound leaves my chest. It's like I have forgotten how to speak.

He has stolen my breath, along with everything else.

A Note from the Author

Dear Reader,

Thank you for joining me for the beginning of Helen's story. This book and the upcoming novels are heavily based on true events from my life, and the lives of several of my close friends. It is very important to me to try to accurately depict Helen's heartache and her struggle to trust someone again and find love after what happened to her.

I have recently been dissatisfied with the depictions of sexual abuse and violence in some popular fiction. I felt it was often used solely as a vehicle for entertainment, and did not truly examine the way that being a victim of such crimes can affect a person's entire life and psyche. I was appalled when someone recently said to me that "only soldiers experience Posttraumatic Stress Disorder," and I discovered that many people think this way. I wanted to try to dispel this common misconception. Almost fifty percent of rapes result in PTSD, and these symptoms can have serious consequences for the sufferer's long-term mental health.

Rape itself is far too common, and it is a problem we face here at home, and in our families; not on some distant battlefield. It also does occur at increased rates for college students like Helen. I find it very upsetting that campuses, which should be sacred places of learning and safe environments, can end up being so dangerous to female students.

Regarding the cliffhanger ending of this story, I must apologize for leaving you without a firm resolution. This book was originally intended to be one single standalone novel, but the more I wrote, the more I fell in love with the characters, and the more it developed into a series. I had planned for Owen to be funny, but he surprised me by being laugh-out-loud hilarious. There was never a boring moment with that character, and I enjoyed writing about him so much that I could do it forever!

After sending the story to my beta-readers for feedback, we all came to the conclusion that this was the best possible place to end the story. It left us with strong lingering thoughts and feelings, that took some time to get past. Rushing into the subsequent events while still recovering from the bombshell Helen just received felt emotionally exhausting. As I wrote the next chapters, I began to realize that the atmosphere had changed greatly and that I was writing an entirely new book that needed to be separated from this one.

I hope that you will join us for the next installment of Clarity, to be released soon! If you enjoyed this novel, it would be a great help if you would take the time to leave a review on Amazon and share your thoughts. You can also join my mailing list to be informed when a new book is available.

Thank you so much for reading!

Best wishes,
Loretta Lost

Loretta Lost

Connect with the author:

Facebook: facebook.com/LorettaLost
Twitter: @LorettaLost
Website: www.LorettaLost.com

Made in the USA
Middletown, DE
11 June 2016